GUNSIGHT

GUNSIGHTS

Elmore Leonard

Thorndike Press • Thorndike, Maine

Library of Congress Cataloging in Publication Data:

Leonard, Elmore, 1925–
 Gunsights.
  1. Large type books. I. Title.
 [PS3562.E55G8 1988]   813'.54   87-33639
 ISBN 0-89621-135-5 (lg. print: alk. paper)

Large Print edition available by arrangement with
H. N. Swanson, Inc., Los Angeles.

Cover design by Bernie Beckman.

For Christopher

Chapter I

The gentleman from *Harper's Weekly,* who didn't know mesquite beans from goat shit, looked up from his reference collection of back issues and said, "I've got it!" Very pleased with himself. "We'll call this affair . . . are you ready? The Early-Moon Feud."

The news reporters in the Gold Dollar shrugged and thought some more, though most of them went on calling it the Rincon Mountains War, which seemed to have enough ring to it.

Somebody said, "What's the matter with the Sweetmary War?" Sweetmary being the name of the mining town where all the gawkers and news reporters had gathered to watch the show. The man from the *St. Louis Globe-Democrat* wanted to call it the Last of The Great Indian Wars. Or – he also mentioned to see how it would sound – the Great Apache Uprising of

1893. Or the Bloody Apache Uprising, etc.

The man from the St. Louis newspaper was reminded that, first, it wasn't an uprising and, second, there weren't just Apache Indians up in the mountains; there were also some niggers. The man from St. Louis, being funny, said, "Well, what if we call it the Last of the Great Indian-Nigger Wars?" A man from Florence said, "Well, you have got the chili-pickers in it also. What about them?" Yes, there were some Mexican settlers too, who had been farming up there a hundred years; they were also involved.

What it was, it was a land war.

The LaSalle Mining Company of New Jersey wanted the land. And the Indians from the White Tanks agency, the colored and the Mexicans — all of them actually living up there — wanted it also.

Dana Moon was the Indian Agent at White Tanks, originally established as a reservation for Warm Springs Apaches, or Mimbreños, and a few Lipan and Tonto-Mojave family groups. The agency was located sixteen miles north of Sweetmary and about the same distance west of the San Pedro River. The reservation land was not in dispute. The problem was, many of Moon's Apaches had wandered away from White Tanks — a bleak, young-desert area — to

8

set up rancherías in the mountains. No one, until now, had complained about it.

Brendan Early worked for LaSalle Mining, sort of, with the title Coordinating Manager, Southwest Region, and was living in Sweetmary at the time.

It was said that he and Dana Moon had been up and down the trail together, had shared dry camps and hot corners, and that was why the *Harper's Weekly* man wanted to call it the Early-Moon Feud; which, as you see, had nothing to do with the heavens or astrology.

Nor was there any personal bitterness between them. The question was: What would happen to their bond of friendship, which had tied them together as though on two ends of a short riata, one not venturing too far without running into the other? Would their friendship endure? Or would they now, holding to opposite principles, cut the riata clean and try to kill one another?

Bringing the land question down to personalities, it presented these two as the star attractions: two well-known, soon-to-be-legendary figures about to butt heads. It brought the crowds to Sweetmary to fill up both hotels, the Congress and the Alamosa, a dozen boarding houses, the seven restaurants and thirteen saloons in town. For several weeks this throng

9

swelled the normal population of about four hundred souls, which included the locals, those engaged in commerce, nearby farmers and ranchers and the miners at the Sweetmary Works. Now there were curiosity seekers, gawkers, from all over the Territory and parts of New Mexico.

(Not here yet were the hundred or more gunmen eventually hired by the company to "protect its leases" and quartered at the mine works. These men were paid, it was said, twenty dollars a week.)

There were newspaper representatives from the *Phoenix Republican, Phoenix Gazette, Yuma Sentinel, Safford Arizonian, Tucson Star, Florence Enterprise, Prescott Courier, Cococino Sun, Clifton Copper Era, Graham County Bulletin, Tombstone Prospector, St. Louis Globe-Democrat, Chicago Times* and the *New York Tribune.*

Harper's Weekly had hired the renowned photographer C.S. Fly of Tombstone to cover the war with his camera, the way he had pictorially recorded Crook's campaign against Geronimo and his renegade Apaches.

C.S. Fly set up a studio on LaSalle Street and there presented "showings" of many of his celebrated photographs of Indians, hangings, memorial parades and well-known personages, including Geronimo, former president Garfield and several of Brendan Early and Dana Moon. The two photos that were perhaps best known showed them at Fort Huachuca, June 16, 1887, with a prisoner they had brought in that day.

There they were, six years ago:

Brendan Early, in his hip-cocked cavalry pose, First Lieutenant of the 10th at Huachuca but wearing civilian dress, a very tight-fitting light-colored suit of clothes; bareheaded to show his brown wavy hair; a silky-looking kerchief at his throat; a matched pair of Smith and Wesson .44 Russians, butt-forward in Army holsters, each with the flap cut off; cavalry boots wiped clean for the pose; Brendan holding his Spencer carbine like a walking cane, palm resting on the upraised barrel. He seems to be trying to look down his nose like an Eastern dandy while suppressing a grin that shows clearly in his eyes.

In contrast:

Dana Moon with his dark, drooping mustache that makes him appear sad; hat brim straight and low over his eyes, a bulge in his bony countenance indicating the ever-present plug of tobacco; dark suit of clothes and a polka-dot neckerchief. Dana's .44 Colt's revolver is in a shoulder rig, a glint of it showing. He grips a Big-fifty Sharps in one hand, a sawed-off 12-gauge Greener in the other. All

11

those guns for a man who looks so mild, so solemn.

Between the two:

Half a head shorter is a one-eyed Mimbreño Apache named Loco. What a funny-looking little man, huh? Black eyepatch, black stringy hair hanging from the bandana covering his head, he looks like a pirate of some kind, wearing an old dirty suitcoat and a loincloth. But don't laugh at him. Loco has killed many people and went to Washington to meet Grover Cleveland when times were better.

The caption beneath the photo, which appeared that year in *Harper's Weekly*, reads:

Lt. Brendan Early Loco Dana Moon
Two Famous Heroes of the West with a Captive
Red Devil

There was also a photo of the Two Famous Heroes standing on either side of an attractive fair-haired young lady in a torn and dirty cotton dress; she is wearing a man's shirt over her quite filthy attire, the shirt unbuttoned, hanging free. The young lady does not seem happy to be posing for her picture that day at Fort Huachuca. She looks as though she might walk up to the camera and kick it over.

12

The caption beneath this one reads:

Lt. Brendan Early   Katherine McKean
Dana Moon
Following Her Ordeal, Kathy McKean
Gratefully Thanks Her Rescuers

In the *Harper's Weekly* article there was mention of a 10th Cavalry sergeant by the name of Bo Catlett, a Negro. Though he did not appear in either of the photographs, Sergeant Catlett had accompanied the Two Famous Heroes in their quest to apprehend the Apache warchief, Loco, and shared credit for bringing him in and rescuing the McKean girl. In the article, Sergeant Catlett was asked where he had gotten the name Bo. "I believe it short for 'Boy,' suh," was his reply.

Not many days before the photographs were taken by C.S. Fly, the five principals involved – Early, Moon, the McKean girl, Loco and Bo Catlett – were down in Old Mexico taking part in an adventure that would dramatically change their lives and, subsequently, lead to the Big Shootout known by most as The Rincon Mountain War.

13

Chapter II

1

St. Helen and Points South: June, 1887
Dana Moon had come down from Whiteriver
to guide for Lieutenant Early and his company
of 10th Cavalry out of Huachuca. They met at
St. Helen, a stage stop on the Hatch & Hodges
Central Mail Section route, where the "massacre" had taken place: the massacre being one
dead swamper, shot several times and his head
shoved into his bucket of axle grease; the driver
of the stage, his shotgun rider and one passenger, a Mr. R. Holmes of St. David. Four were
dead; two passengers caught in the gunfire and
wounded superficially; and one passenger ab-
ducted, Miss Katherine McKean of Benson, on
her way home from visiting kin in Tucson.

Loco was recognized as the leader of the

raiding party (How many one-eyed Apaches were there between San Carlos and Fort Huachuca?) and was last seen trailing due south toward the Whetstone Mountains, though more likely was heading for the San Pedro and open country: Loco, the McKean girl and about twenty others in the band that had jumped the reservation a few days before.

"Or about ten," Dana Moon said. "Those people" – meaning Apaches – "can cause you to piss your britches and see double."

Brendan Early, in his dusty blues, looked at the situation, staring south into the sun haze and heat waves, looking at nothing. But Brendan Early was in charge here and had to give a command.

What did they have? In the past month close to 150 Warm Springs people had jumped the San Carlos reservation, women and children as well as bucks, and made a beeline down the San Pedro Valley to Old Mexico and the fortress heights of the Sierra Madres. Loco's bunch was the rear guard, gathering fresh mounts and firearms along the way. Maybe Bren Early's troopers could ride like wild men a day and a night, killing some horses and maybe, just maybe, cut Loco off at the crossing.

Or, a lieutenant in the U.S. Cavalry might ride through the scrub and say, "What border?"

even after ten years on frontier station, cross leisurely with extra mounts and do the job.

Dana Moon — sent down here by Al Sieber, Chief of Scouts at San Carlos — waited, not giving the lieutenant any help. He sat his chestnut gelding, looking down from there with the tobacco wad in his jaw. He didn't spit; he didn't do a thing.

While Lieutenant Early was thinking, Then what? Track the renegades, run 'em to ground? Except his troop of U.S. Cavalry would be an invading army, wouldn't it? having crossed an international boundary contrary to treaty agreement and the mutual respect of foreign soil, customs, emigration, all that bullshit.

"Lord Jehovah protect us from dumb-ass officialdom," said the lieutenant out loud to no one in particular.

All soil west of the Pecos looked the same to Bren Early — born and raised in Monroe, Michigan (adopted home of George Armstrong Custer), before matriculating at West Point, somehow getting through, one hundred seventy-ninth in a class of one ninety-two — and there was no glory standing around a wagon yard watching civilians bleed.

Dana Moon read sign — grain shucks in horse shit, and could tell you where the rider had come from how long ago — and sometimes

16

he could read Bren Early's mind. He said, "You're gonna hurt your head thinking. You want to do it, I'll take you four and a half days' ride southwest, yes, across the line toward Morelos, and on the sixth day Loco and his fellas will ride up to our camp. But not with all your troopers. You and me and Bo Catlett to handle the cavvy if he wants to come, six months on the string, grain and water. If you don't want to do it I think I'll quit government work; I'm tired looking over the fence and watching dust settle."

"On the sixth day," Bren Early said, nodding. "And on the seventh day we'll rest, huh?"

He bought the tight-fitting suit of clothes off the St. Helen station agent for seven dollars, and for three more got Bo Catlett a coat, vest and derby hat. Hey, boy, they were going to Old Mexico like three dude tourists:

Rode southeast and crossed into Sonora at dusk, guided by the faint lights of a border town, against the full-dark moonside of the sky.

2

Dana Moon's plan: ride straight for a well he knew would be on Loco's route; get down there in the neighborhood, scout the rascal and his band to make sure they were coming; then, when they arrived, parley with the thirsty renegades, keeping their guns between the Apaches and a drink of water. Talk them out of the McKean girl first — if she was still alive — then talk about the weather or whatever they wanted, gradually getting the discussion around to a return trip to San Carlos for everybody, all expenses paid.

Or commence firing when they draw within range, Bren Early thought, seeing it written up as a major skirmish or, better yet, the Battle of . . . whatever the name of this rancho used to be, sitting in the scrub oak foothills: three weathered adobes in a row like a small garrison, mesquite-pole outbuilding and corral, part of an adobe wall enclosing the yard.

Out fifty yards of worn-out pasture was a windmill rigged to a stock tank of scummy water. From the end house or the wall, three men could cover the tank and a thirsty traveler would have to get permission to drink if the three men didn't want him to.

The Battle of Rancho Diablo. Give it a hellfire exciting name. Who'd know the difference?

On the sixth day Dana Moon rode in from his early-morning scout, field glasses hanging on his chest. He said, "What ever happens the way you expect it to?" He did spit right then.

Bren Early saw it. He said, "Duty at Huachuca."

"They split up," Dana Moon told him and Bo Catlett. "It looks to be Loco and the young lady coming ahead. They'll be here by noon, the ones with the herd maybe an hour behind. And some more dust coming out of the west."

"Federales," Bo Catlett said.

"Not enough of 'em," Moon said. "Some other party; maybe eight or ten."

They brought the spare horses and feed into the middle adobe, three saddled horses into the building closest to the stock-tank end of the yard, and went inside to wait.

Hoofprints out there meant nothing; people came through here all times of the year traveling between Morelos and Bavispe and points beyond, this being the gateway to the Sierra Madres.

Still, when Loco came, leading the second horse and rider they took to be the girl, he hung back 300 yards – the horses straining toward the smell of water – and began to circle as he approached the rancho again, coming around through the pasture now, keeping the wall between him and the adobes.

"We'll have to wing him," Bren Early said,

flat against the wall with his Spencer, next to a front window.

Moon watched through the slit opening in the wooden door. He said to Bo Catlett, "Mount up."

Bo Catlett did and had to remain hunched over in the McClellan, his derby hat grazing the low roof.

"That one-eyed Indian is a little speck of a target, isn't he?" Bren Early said.

"Tired and thirsty," Moon said. "I'm going out." He looked up at Bo Catlett. "He flushes when he sees me, run him down. There won't be any need to shoot."

Bren Early, dropping the stock of his Spencer to the dirt floor, said, "Shit. And parley awhile." He didn't like it; then thought of something and squinted out past the window frame again.

"I wonder what that girl looks like," he said. "I wonder what the one-eyed son of a bitch's been doing to her."

Moon said, "Probably looks at her and thinks the same thing you would." He glanced up to see Bo Catlett showing his yellow-white teeth, grinning at him, and Moon thought of his mother telling him a long time ago why colored people had good, strong teeth: because they ate cold leftovers in the kitchen and couldn't afford to buy candy and things that weren't good for you.

Outside, Moon raised his arm. He saw Loco stop about a hundred yards off: the Apache deciding how much he wanted water or if he could win a race if he turned and ran. He saw the roan horse behind coming up next to Loco – yes, blond hair stirring, the McKean girl. Then saw something he didn't expect: the girl twisting in her saddle and shoving the Apache hard with both hands, sending him off his horse to land hard and lie there a moment while the girl reached to unhitch the lead line from the Indian's saddle; and now she was kicking her roan out of there, not bothering to look back as Moon yelled at her, "Wait! . . . Hey, come on back!" Then turning, getting out of the way as he called to Bo, "Get her!"

Bo Catlett came out of the door chute, chin pressed into the horse's mane, rose up in the yard and pressed down again as the horse cleared the four-foot adobe wall – Loco standing now, watching for a moment, then gathering his reins and coming on, not interested in the two horses racing across the pasture toward a haze of mountains.

They sat inside the doorway of the house with no furniture: Dana Moon and Loco with cups of sweet black coffee, the square of outside light between them on the earth floor. Bren Early came over from the fireplace where the coffee pot sat on a sheet of tin over the smoldering mesquite sticks. He stood looking out the window that was behind the Apache.

Loco said in Spanish, "Tell him I don't like him there."

Moon looked up at Bren. "He asks you to join us."

"Tell him he smells."

Moon motioned to him. "Come on, be sociable." To Loco he said in Spanish, "So, here we are."

Squatting down, Bren Early said, "Ask him, for Christ sake, what he did to the girl."

The Apache's one eye shifted. "Did to her? Did what?" he said in English.

"Is she all right?" asked Moon.

"She needs to be beaten," the Apache said. "Maybe cut off the end of her nose."

"Jesus Christ," Bren Early said. He got up and stepped to the window again.

"He speaks of Hey-soo Cristo." The Apache

paused and said, using Spanish again, "What is the matter he can't sit down?"

"He wants to do battle," Moon said.

The Apache stretched open his one eye, raising his brow as if to shrug. "Wouldn't it be good if we could have what we want? I take all the mountains sunrise of the river San Pedro. You take all your people and go back to Washington" — pronouncing it Wasi-tona — "be by your big chief, Grover Cleveland. Man, he was very fat, do you know it?"

"He eats good," Moon said.

"Yes, but he gave us nothing. We sat in a room in chairs. He didn't seem to know why we were there."

"You liked Washington?" asked Moon.

"Good water there," Loco said, "but no country or mountains that I saw. Now they are sending our people to Fort Sill in Okla-homa. Is it like Washington?"

"I don't know," Moon said. "*He* served there one time," looking up at Bren Early.

"I believe it," the Apache said.

"It's like San Carlos, but with more people and houses."

"With mountains?"

"I don't think so," Moon said. "I've never been there. I've never been to Washington either. I've been to Sonora . . . Santa Fe, in the

New Mexico Territory."

"The buildings in Washington are white," Loco said. "There are men made of iron on horses also made of iron. Many buildings and good water. You should go there and live if that's what your people like."

"I like mountains, as you do," Moon said. "I was born here, up on Oak Creek. I want to stay here, the same as you do. But there's a difference. They say, 'Put Loco and his people on the train to Fort Sill.' I can say, 'Put him on yourself, I won't do it.' And somebody puts you on the train. It's too bad, but what can I do about it?"

"Jesus Christ," Bren Early said, listening to them talking so seriously and understanding the drift but not the essence of what they were saying and feeling.

Moon raised his eyes, "We're looking at the situation."

Bren Early made a gun out of his right index finger, aimed it at the back of Loco's head and said, "Pow. That's how you solve it. You two're chatting — last week he shot four people dead. So we send him to Oklahoma for a vacation."

"It's the high part of his life to raid and steal horses, since the first Spaniard came up this valley," Moon said. "What else does he know?

24

What's right and what's wrong on his side of the fence?"

"My life is to meet the hostile enemy and destroy him," Bren said. "That's what I know."

"Listen to yourself," Moon said. "You want a war, go find one." He began gathering Spanish words again and said to Loco, "When your men arrive, tell them to get all of your people here in the mountains and bring them back to San Carlos. You go with us. It's the way it has to be for right now."

"Maybe it won't be so easy," Loco said. "There are others coming too."

Yes, the dust from the west, eight or ten riders. "Who are they?" Moon asked.

Loco touched the dirty red pirate bandana covering his head. "The ones who take hair."

"You're sure of it?"

"If they're not of you, or not the soldiers of Mexico, who are they?" the Apache said.

4

Bo Catlett came back with Katy McKean, the girl eyeing them with suspicion as she rode into the yard, sitting her roan like they'd have to pull her off it. Then sitting up there feeling left out, because they didn't have time for her those first moments. Bo Catlett began telling them about the riders coming. He said it looked like they had scattered the Indian herd and the two sides had exchanged gunfire, Bo Catlett hearing the reports in the distance. Now some of them for sure, if not all, were coming this way and it wouldn't be too long before they'd see the dust.

Bren Early studied the girl as he listened, thinking to himself, My, my, my, the poor sweet young thing all dirty and tattered, like the savages had rolled her on the ground and torn at her dress to get it off.

He said, "Miss," helping her down, taking her by the arm, "come on inside out of the hot sun." She pulled her arm away, giving him a mean look, and Bren said, "What're you mad at *me* for? I just want to give you some coffee."

"I ain't going in there with him," the McKean girl said, looking at Loco standing in the doorway. "Less you want to loan me one of your guns."

"Don't worry," Bren said. "He gets familiar with you again, I'll make the little heathen marry you. But how are you, all things being equal?"

The girl said, "What do you mean *again?*"

"I was just teasing," Bren said, "showing you

26

there's nothing to worry about."

"He tried things," the McKean girl said. "I hit him in his good eye and kicked him up under his skirt where it'd do the most good. But I ain't going in that room with him. I still got his smell in my nose."

Dana Moon took her gently by the arm. She looked at him but didn't resist as he said in his quiet tone, "You been through something, lady, I know; and we're going to watch over you."

"Thank you," the girl said, subdued.

"But you got to do what I tell you for the time being, you understand? You can kick and scream when you get home, but right now try and act nice."

5

Who were they?, was the question: Watching from the windows as they had waited for the Indian, Moon and Bren Early with their glasses on the riders raising dust across the old pasture.

"Seven, eight," Bren Early said. "Like cowpunchers heading for town."

"Starting to hang back, sniff the air," Dana Moon said. What did those people out there know, looking this way? First, trailing Apaches with a horse herd and a white woman. Then, seeing a man in a derby hat riding off with her. They would have to be confused.

"They traded shots," Bren Early said and paused, thinking, Then what? "If they wanted the horses, why didn't they take 'em?"

Which was about where Moon was in his own mind. "Say they did, and left somebody with the herd. How many you count, Bo?"

"Ten," Bo Catlett said. "Coulda been another one."

"And they saw you for sure."

"Couldn't miss us — time I got the lady turned around."

"They're cowhands," the McKean girl said, with that edge to her tone again, not feeling very rescued crowded into this adobe room with four men and animals. She had moved up by Moon's window and stood close to him, seeing the hard bump in his jaw, wondering if he would ever spit; then would look over at Bren Early, maybe admiring his long wavy hair, or the tight, shrunk-looking suit molded to his tall frame. Squinting out the window, she said, "You can tell by the look of them, the way they ride."

Still, the McKean girl had to admit — without saying it aloud — it was a bunch of riders for not having any cows, and moving south at that, not like they were heading home from a drive.

"There was a man used to sell us beef at San Carlos," Moon said. "I believe the name was Sundeen." Still watching through his glasses, seeing the the riders at four hundred yards now, spreading out more as they came at a choppy walk, not a sound from them yet.

"I used to know him," the McKean girl said, a little surprised.

Maybe they didn't hear her. Bo Catlett said, "The same man supplied meat to Huachuca. Look in his war-bag you see a running iron, it's Phil Sundeen. Used to bring his beef in vented every which way; cows look like somebody was learning to write on 'em."

Moon said, "If I remember — hired vaqueros he paid twenty a month and feed. And we see some Mexican hats, don't we?"

"Which one's Sundeen?" Bren Early asked.

As Moon studied the bunch through his glasses, the McKean girl, squinting, said, "That stringy one on the sorrel — I bet he's got a hatband made of silver conchas."

"Something there's catching the light," Moon said.

"And forty-fours in crossed belts with silver buckles?"

"You got him," Moon said.

"Don't anybody listen to me," the McKean girl said. "I used to know him when his dad was still running things, before they sent Phil Sundeen to Yuma prison."

"That's the one," Moon said. "You knew him, huh?"

"I was ac*quainted* with him," the McKean girl said. "I wasn't to have nothing to do with him and that was fine with me. He was cheeky, loud and had ugly ways about him."

Bren Early said, "What was he in prison for?"

"As this colored man said, for using his running iron freely," the McKean girl answered. "It might be he run a herd down here to the Mexicans. On the way home he sees One-Eye here and decides to go for the bounty trade. Ask the Indian. He wouldn't have given himself up otherwise, would he?"

The men in the adobe room looked at this girl who seemed to know what she was talking about. How old? Still in her twenties, a healthy-looking girl, though dirty and sun-burned at the moment. Yes, she knew a few hard facts of life.

Bren Early, leaning against the wall by his window, looked from the girl to Loco. "You must be worth plenty, all these people bush, looking everywhere but at Moon and Early until he was about thirty feet from the adobe wall, then giving them a surprised look: like, what're you doing here?

The riders back of him, small figures, stood around while their horses watered in the corrugated tank and in the slough that had formed from seepage. One of the figures – it looked to be Sundeen – had his peter out and was taking a leak facing this way: telling them what he thought of the situation.

The Mexican touched his hat, loosening it and setting it again. Even with the revolver on his leg and the cartridge belt across his chest he seemed friendly standing there.

He said, "Good afternoon. How are you today?"

Moon and Bren Early watched him, Bren murmuring, "Jesus Christ," under his breath.

"It's good to reach water on a hot day," the Mexican said. "Have you been here very long?"

Moon and Bren Early seemed patient, waiting for him to get to it.

"We looking for friends of ours," the Mexican said. "We wonder if you see anybody ride by here the past hour."

Bren Early said, "Haven't seen a soul."

The Mexican took time to look past them study the adobes, seeing the white smoke

coming to see you."

"Make 'em bid high," the McKean girl said, "and look at the scrip before you hand him over, or that son of a bitch Sundeen will try and cheat you."

The men in the room had to look at that girl again.

Moon saw the waiting expression in Loco's eye and said, "He ain't going with them, he's going home."

"I know he's going home," Bren Early said. "I didn't come six days for the ride."

"If it means an argument, what difference does it make who takes him?" the McKean girl asked. She was serious.

Bren Early said, "Because he belongs to me, that's why."

And Moon said to her, going over to his horse, "I'll try and explain it to you sometime."

Bren Early was watching the riders, two hundred yards now, still coming spread out. "We got blind sides in here," he said. "Let's get out to the wall."

Moon was bringing a spare revolver out of his saddle bag, a Smith & Wesson .38 double-action model. He said, "You don't mean everybody."

Bren Early looked at him. "I'm referring to you and me only. Shouldn't that do the job?"

Moon pulled his sawed-off Greener from inside his blanket roll. Coming back to the window he handed the .38 to the McKean girl, saying, "You don't have to cock it, just keep pulling on the trigger's the way it works. But let me tell you something." Moon paused, looking at the Apache only a few feet away. "He's with us, you understand? He's ours. Nobody else's." Moon looked at Bo Catlett then and said, "Bo, give him his gun. Soon as it's over, take it back."

Walking out to the adobe wall, carrying their firearms, they watched the riders coming on, the riders looking this way but cutting an angle toward the stock tank.

"We'll let 'em water," Bren Early said.

"You give 'em too much they'll camp there," Moon said.

"We got no choice but have a talk first, do we?"

"No," Moon said.

"So they'll water and stretch first, take a pee and look the situation over. I hope they don't use dirty language and offend the girls ears."

"Don't worry about *her*," Moon said.

He laid his Greener on the chest-high crumbling wall, leaned the Sharps against it, cocked, in front of him, loosened the Colt's in his shoulder rig, then decided to take his coat off:

folded it neatly and laid it on the wall a few feet away.

"They're watching us," he said.

"I hope so," Bren Early said.

Bren had leaned his Spencer against the adobe wall. Now he drew his big .44 S & W Russians, broke each one open to slide a bullet into the empty sixth chamber and reholstered his guns.

Sundeen's bunch was at the stock tank now, fifty yards off, stepping down from the saddles.

Bren Early said, "At Chancellorsville, a Major Peter Keenan took his Eighth Pennsylvania Cavalry, four hundred men and — buying time for the artillery to set up — charged them full against ten thousand Confederate infantry. Talk about odds."

Moon turned his head a little. "What happened to 'em?"

"They all got killed."

6

The Mexican in the straw Chihu[...] who came over to talk looked at first [...] out for a stroll, squinting up at the [...] at the haze of mountains, inspec[...]

rising from the first chimney and vanishing in the glare.

"Where your horses?"

"Out of the sun," Bren Early said.

"You good to them," the Mexican said. "What else you got in there?"

"Troop of cavalry," Bren Early said and called out, "Sergeant!"

Bo Catlett, with a Spencer, appeared in the doorway of the first adobe, calling back, "Suh!"

The Mexican began to shake his head very slowly. "You got the Uninah States Army in there? Man, I like to see that." His gaze returned to Bren Early and Moon. "Soldiers . . . but you don't have no uniforms on." He paused. "You don't want nobody to know you here, huh? Listen, we won't tell nobody."

"You don't know what you've seen, what you haven't seen," Bren Early said. "Leave it at that."

The Mexican said, "You don't want to invite me in there?"

Moon drew his Colt from the shoulder rig and put it on the Mexican. "You got a count of three to move out of here," he said. "One . . . two . . . three – "

"*Éspere*," the Mexican said. "Wait. It's all right with me." He began to back away, his gaze holding on Moon's revolver. "You don't want to

35

be friends, all right, maybe some other time. Good afternoon to you."

7

The Mexican, whose name was Ruben Vega, forty-four years of age, something like seven to ten years older than the two men at the wall, said to himself, Never again. Going there like that and acting a fool. Good afternoon. How are you today? They knew, those two. They knew what was going on and weren't buying any of that foolish shit today. Never again, Ruben Vega said to himself again, walking back to the stock tank . . . Sundeen waiting for him.

Sundeen with his eyes creased in the sun glare, pulling the funneled brim of his hat down lower.

"He was bluffing you. Don't you know when a man's bluffing?" Like the joke was on Ruben Vega and Sundeen had seen through it right away.

"Sometimes I don't see the bluff if the man's good at it," Ruben Vega said. "These two mean it. Why is it worth it to them?, I don't know. But they mean it."

"Eight to three," Sundeen said. "What difference is it what they mean?, the Indin's ours."

"I don't know," Ruben Vega said, shaking his head. "You better talk to them yourself."

Sundeen wasn't listening now. He was squinting past the Mexican and touching his two-week's growth of beard, fondling it, caressing himself, as he studied the pair of figures at the wall. One of them had yelled, "Sergeant," and the booger had stuck his head out. Soldiers — chased after the Apache and now had him in there. That part was clear enough. The girl, she must be in there, too. But eight guns against three was what it came to. So what was the problem? Ask for the Apache. Ask at gunpoint if need be. Those people would have no choice but to hand him over and be happy to do it.

He said to the Mexican, "Send two around back to make 'em nervous. The rest of us'll walk in." The Mexican didn't say anything and Sundeen looked at him. "What's the matter?"

"It isn't the way to do it."

Sundeen looked at the Mexican's old-leather face, at the thick, tobacco-stained mustache covering his mouth and the tiny blood lines in his tired-looking eyes.

"You're getting old, you know it?"

"I think that's it," Ruben Vega said. "I'm getting old because I'm still alive."

Sundeen wanted to push him and say, God-damn it, quit kicking dirt and come on; there's nothing to this. But he knew Ruben Vega pretty well. He paid him fifty dollars a month because Ruben Vega was good with men, even white men, and was one trail-wise first-class segundo to have riding point with a herd of rustled stock, or tracking after a loose Apache with a Mexican price on his head. Like the one-eyed Mimbre, Loco: 2,000 pesos, dead or alive.

When Ruben Vega spoke, Sundeen generally paid attention. But this time – Ruben had been bluffed out, was all, and was trying to save his face, sound wise, like he knew something as fact; whereas it was just an off-day for him and his back ached or his piles were bothering him.

Sundeen looked over at his riders, part of them hunkered down in the stingy shade of the stock tank: four Americans and two skinny Mexicans with their heavy crisscrossed gun-belts. He said to Ruben Vega, "I'll show you how white men do it," grinning a little. "I'll send your two boys around back where it's safe, and march in with the rest of these ugly bronc stompers myself."

"I'll watch you," Ruben Vega said.

Sundeen looked over at the riders again,

38

saying, "Who wants to earn a month's wages this fine afternoon?"

8

"Now we're getting to it," Bren Early said, seeing the five men assembling, starting to come out from the tank, spreading out in a line. "I don't see a rifle amongst them; so they intend to come close, don't they?" And told himself not to talk so much, or else Dana would think he was nervous.

"The other two," Dana Moon said. "Leaving or what?"

Two with Mexican hats, mounted, were moving away from the tank, off to the right, heading out into the scrub.

"Do we want them behind us?"

"Uh-unh," Bren Early said. He picked up his Spencer as Moon hefted his Sharps, watching the two Mexicans riders swinging wide, going out to nearly two hundred yards as they began to circle at a gallop.

"The horses first," said Moon, "if that's agreeable."

"I suppose," the cavalryman answered,

"but it's a shame."

"If they keep coming, you finish it. I'll tend to the others."

Moon stole a look at the five on foot coming out from the tank, taking their time, one remaining back there with the horses.

He said, "When you're ready."

They pressed Spencer and Sharps to their shoulders and almost instantly the hard, heavy reports came **BAM**-BAM in the stillness and the two running horses two hundred yards out stumbled and went down with their riders in sudden burts of dust, the tiny figures flying, tumbling.

Moon turned his empty Sharps on the line of five, saw them stop dead.

Bren Early called, "Sergeant!"

Moon didn't look around. He heard off behind him, "Suh!" And Bren Early calmly, "Two on the flank. Keep 'em there. They move, shoot 'em." And the black voice saying, "Suh!" and that was done.

The five had broken line and were looking out that way, losing some of their starch maybe. But the one with crossed gunbelts and silver buckles was saying something, getting them back in business and they were coming again, the line of men about fifteen feet wide — Sundeen in the middle — every one of them shaggy and scruffy, rannies with hard squints trying to look mean, and they did.

The last exchange made between Moon and Bren Early was Moon saying, "If it comes to it, work from the ends," and Bren Early saying, "And meet at the silver buckles."

Now the floor was Sundeen's, bringing his line to a halt at a distance Moon's eyes measured as a long stride short of forty feet. A good working range: close enough for a sawed-off, far enough you'd have to aim a revolver if you had nerve enough to take the time. Who were these brush poppers? Were they any good? Moon and Bren Early were about to find out.

Sundeen said to the two at the wall, "Are you nervous or something? We come to talk to you is all."

He waited a moment, but they didn't say anything. Then looked off into the distance at the two dead horses and the riders stranded out there before bringing his gaze back to the wall.

"Like shooting a buck, that range. I guess you've done it in your time. But here looking at it close to earth is different, huh? You see what you got on your hands? Now then," Sundeen said, "you also got that red nigger in there by the name of Loco we want you to hand over to us. Do you see a reason to discuss it any?"

"He's mine," Bren Early said. "He

41

goes home with me."

"Oh, are you the gent in charge?" asked Sundeen. "Then tell me something. What difference does it make who takes this Indin, long as we rid the earth of him?"

"I was sent to get him," Bren Early said, "and I did."

"A long piece from home without your uniform on, soldier boy. I bet you shouldn't even be 'cross the border here. What I'm saying, it looks like I got more right to the red nigger than you have. I got the law on my side."

"But I've got the Indian," Bren Early said. "What remains is how dearly you want to pay for him."

"Turn it around," Sundeen said. "Why would you put up your life to keep him? I'm gonna ride out with him, one way or the other."

Moon said then, "You ever mount up again you'll do it bleeding to death."

Sundeen shook his head. What was the matter with these two? — and had to make himself calm down. He said, "Listen to us grown men arguing over a little one-eyed Indin."

"What's he worth," asked Moon, "couple thousand pesos?"

"Sure, there's something in it, or we wouldn't be talking," Sundeen answered. "But you can't hand him in and collect the bounty, not if

42

you're U.S. Army. They find out back home, they'll cut your buttons off, won't they? Drum you out. It may be duty with you, if you say it is; but it's pure business with me. Way to make a living." Sundeen paused. He said then, "It gives me an idea. What we might do is divvy him up. You give me his hair and his eye patch, something to identify him to the Mex gover'ment, and you take the rest of him back where you came from. And if that ain't a deal I never heard one."

Sundeen glanced both ways at the pair of riders on either side of him, then looked at the two behind the low wall again, pleased with himself, his display of wisdom and generosity.

Bren Early did not stop and think a moment. Yes, if they'd had to shoot the Indian they'd be bringing him back dead anyway. But how would they explain his tonsured head, the scalplock ripped from his skull? Then realized, No, that wasn't the point at all. It was a question of principle, beyond reason or even good sense. A question of standing at the drawn line and never backing off.

Bren Early said to Moon, but for all to hear, "Do you want to tell him to stick it in his horse, or should I?"

Sundeen was a grunt away from giving in to his violent nature; but knew his men had to look at him or hear him and all of them pull at the same time to do the job right. Put the two off guard and then hit. It wasn't going the way he thought it would – that goddamn Ruben Vega telling him, knowing something. With the hook still in his belly but holding on to good judgment, Sundeen said, "I'm gonna go talk to my partner a minute. See if we can think of a way to satisfy us."

Moon and Bren Early watched him turn away from them, his rannies looking at him like, What's going on? Sundeen dropping a word as he glanced left and right, all of them moving off now.

Bren said, "He's used to having his way."

Moon said, "But he didn't come prepared, did he?"

"I'll give them three more steps," Bren said and pulled his matched Smith & Wesson .44's. Moon drew his Colt's, gathered the sawed-off Greener from the wall in his left hand.

Three more strides – that was it.

The five came around with weapons in their hands, Sundeen hollering something, and his two men on the ends fell dead in the first sudden explosion from the wall, before they were full around, Bren Early and Moon with revolvers extended, aiming, firing at the scattering, snap-shooting line, Bren holding both the

44

big .44 Russians out in front of him and moving his head right and left to look down the barrels and fire; Moon holding the Greener low against its hard buck and letting go a Double-O charge at a half-kneeling figure and seeing the man's arm fly up with the big-bore report, swinging the Greener on Sundeen and raking his boots with a charge as Sundeen stumbled and Bren Early fired, shooting his hat off, firing again and seeing the man let go of his revolvers and grab his face with both hands as he sank to the ground.

They went over the wall and walked out to where the five lay without moving.

"Four dead," Bren Early said.

Moon nodded. "For no reason. This one looks to be right behind."

Sundeen was still alive, lying in the sun as his life drained from shotgun wounds in both legs, bullet wounds in his neck, through his left cheek and where part of his left ear had been shot away.

Ruben Vega came out to them, looking at the men on the ground. He said, "Well, I tried to tell him."

The Mexican began to think of how he would get Sundeen to Morelos, or if he should try; and if he should take the others over their horses or leave them here. He walked around them, nudging one and then another with his boot, making sure they were dead; then began to recite the names of these men, as though saying last words over them:

Lonnie Baker.

Clement Hurd.

Dick Maddox.

Jack McWilliams.

Moon and Bren Early heard him, but they were looking toward the adobe now, seeing the girl and the sergeant and the Indian in the yard, and they didn't listen to the names carefully and store them away. It could have helped them later if they did.

Chapter III

1

When the news reporters first came here to cover the War they had to look for the "angle." The Big Company trying to run off the little homesteaders was good stuff; they could write it as factually as need be from both sides. But it would be far better if Personalities were involved: names of newsworthy individuals that readers would recognize, or, feel dumb if they didn't after the news articles described their colorful and exciting past histories.

What could you do with William A. Vandozen, the LaSalle Mining vice-president who was completely lacking in color, appeared in town once in a while but would not talk to anyone when he did?

What kind of story would you get from an

47

Apache Indian homesteader named Iskay-mon-ti-zah who didn't speak English anyway?

This was, in part, the reason Dana Moon and Brendan Early were elected to be the principal antagonists, bound to come together sooner or later, which would be the climax, the Big Story: two living legends in a fight to the finish.

Fine, the editors of the newspapers would wire back to their reporters. But who are they? What did they do? GET TO WORK AND DIG UP SOME BACKGROUND! was the tone of the wires if not the actual words.

The news reporters hanging out at the Gold Dollar would shake their heads. Just like a goddamn editor — like asking what Wild Bill Hickok did for a living. (What *did* he do? No one asked.) They all nodded their heads in agreement as to editors.

All right, they'd go talk to the principals involved.

But try to get a straight answer from Brendan Early who was stuck-up, high-and-mighty, vain and rude when interviewed. They would ask him questions such as: "What is it like to kill a man?" He would stare back at them and not answer. "Do you think you will die by the gun?" Answer: "If you don't leave, somebody will." Or they would ask a question in a group

48

none would dare ask alone: "What turned you against humanity?" The famous Bren Early: "Pains in the ass like you people." They would see him drinking whiskey and playing faro, then not see him for days while he remained holed-up in his room in the Congress Hotel or visited the mysterious Mrs. Pierson who lived in a house on Mill Street without any visible means of support.

Or try to locate Dana Moon, having to go all the way up into the mountains on a two-day pack. Finally, there he was. Ask him a list of shrewd questions and have him say, "You people don't know what you're talking about, do you?"

So the reporters filed embroidered stories based on hearsay and sketchy information they accepted as fact. They wrote that Bren Early had been court-martialed following the Sonora Incident and cashiered out of the Army. Since then he had been:

A hunting guide.

Road agent.

Convict in a work gang.

Gold prospector.

Had shot and killed anywhere from ten to twenty men.

All this before selling his claim to LaSalle Mining and joining the company. Great stuff, plenty of material here to work with.

Dana Moon's background wasn't as colorful, though it was solid ground to build on. After Sonora he had been fired from his position as Assistant Supervisor, San Carlos Indian Reservation, and had entered the business of mustanging: supplying remounts to Fort Huachuca and stage horses to Hatch & Hodges, before they shut down their lines. He was known to be a rough customer who had shot and killed a few men himself. Now, and for the past few years, Dana Moon was in charge of the Apache subagency at White Tanks.

Yes, Moon and Early had crossed paths several times since the Sonora Incident, which is what made the "angle" of these two eventually tearing into each other a natural. Headlines, with facts slightly bent, practically wrote themselves.

PERSONAL FEUD SETS STAGE FOR LAND FIGHT

MOON AND EARLY FACTIONS LINE UP
FOR BATTLE

Great stuff.

While all the "color" was being written, a young *Chicago Times* journalist by the name of

50

Maurice Dumas, who had not yet mastered a pose of cynicism or world-weariness, did talk to both Bren Early and Dana Moon. Young Maurice Dumas asked straight questions and didn't know any better when he got direct answers.

Beginners luck, the other news reporters said.

2

Was it luck? Or the fact Maurice Dumas had trained himself to jump out of bed each day at 6:30 A.M. and immediately check his list of THINGS TO DO. At seven he walked into the Congress Hotel dining room and there was Brendan Early, alone: the first time Maurice Dumas had ever seen the man without a crowd around him.

"Excuse me, but would you mind if I interviewed you?" Nervous as hell.

Brendan Early looked up from his T-bone steak, tomatoes and scrambled eggs. He looked different than he did in the C.S. Fly photos: his face was thinner and he now wore a heavy mustache that curved down around his mouth and was darker than his hair.

51

"Let me hear your first question."

"Well — were you chucked out of the Army or did you retire?"

"You mean you are asking instead of telling me?" Brendan Early said. "Sit down."

Both surprised and encouraged, Maurice Dumas took off his cap and did as he was told. He couldn't believe it.

"I quit, resigned my commission," Bren Early said.

"What did you do right after that?"

"I rested."

"Thought of what you would do next?"

"Thought of staying alive. I thought quite a lot about it."

"Meaning you had to make a living?"

"I thought of ladies somewhat. But most often I thought of staying alive."

"I believe you advertised your services to lead western hunting expeditions. In Chicago and other eastern papers?"

"It's true. The advertisements said, 'Ladies welcome . . . Your dear lady will be well protected and taken care of.' "

"How long were you a hunting guide?"

"I wasn't a guide, I *hired* guides to do the work while I led the expeditions."

"How long did you do that?"

"Till I got tired of smiling."

The news reporter wasn't sure he understood that; but he preferred to cover ground rather than clear up minor points. He watched Mr. Early take a silver flask from inside his dark suitcoat and pour a good slug into his coffee.

"Is that whiskey?"

"Cognac. I don't drink whiskey in the morning."

"May I continue?"

"Please do."

"It's said you've killed between ten and twenty men. How many exactly did you?"

"That's not the question to ask."

Maurice Dumas thought a moment. "Did you know their names?"

And saw Mr. Early pause over his breakfast and look at him with interest.

"That's the question. How did you know to ask it?"

"It seemed like a good one," the reporter said.

Brendan Early nodded, saying, "It's interesting that some of them — I don't mean the back-shooters, of course — would announce themselves with the sound of death in their tone. 'Mr. Early . . . I am R.J. Baker.' Then stare with a hard, solemn look, like I was supposed to faint or piss my britches."

"Really? What happened that time? The one said his name was Baker?"

53

"Don't you want some breakfast?"

"I'll just have some of this coffee, if I may."

Eating his steak, watching the young reporter pour himself a cup from the silver pot on the table Brendan Early said, "Are you sure you're from a newspaper? You aren't like the rest of that snotty bunch at all."

"*Chicago Times*," Maurice Dumas said. "There are so many things I want to ask you about." Including the mysterious Mrs. Pierson, who lived over on Mill Street. Was she just a friend or what?

"Don't be nervous." Brendan Early looked through the doors to the railroad clock in the hall. "We got till I get tired of talking or you decide you know more than I do. This morning I'm going shooting."

"You mean — up there?"

"No, I'm gonna step out into the desert and limber up my revolvers and test my eyesight."

"Getting ready for the showdown," Maurice Dumas said, squirming in his chair a little.

"You're starting to sound like the others," Brendan Early said. "Don't tell me things. Ask me."

"I'm sorry. How come you're going out to limber up your revolvers?"

"Today and tomorrow. I intend to shoot off several boxes of forty-fours. Because sometime

54

soon, I've been told, an acquaintance from long ago will arrive in Benson by train, get here somehow or other, and I don't know his present frame of mind."

"You mean somebody who wants to kill you?"

"Ask him that one. Fella by the name of Phil Sundeen, come back from the dead."

Maurice Dumas frowned. What was going on? He said, "Sundeen. I don't believe I've heard that name before."

"Well, write it down. It could be an item for your paper."

Chapter IV

1

Dragoon Mountains: April, 1888

The smell of the mares was on the wind, but the stud did not seem to like this graze as a place to breed. He lowered his head, giving the signal, and the mares and the stallions skitting around them followed after as the lead mare moved off.

Seven days Dana Moon had been tracking this herd, gradually, patiently moving the wild horses toward a barranca they'd fenced off with brush; a week of watching, getting to know them, Moon thinking on and off: If you were the stud, which one would you pick to mount first?

It would be hard. There were some good-looking mares in that bunch. But each time he wondered about it Moon found his gaze cutting out the palomino, the golden-haired girl, from the rest of the mares. She attracted the most overtures from the stallions who'd come sniffing her flanks. Moon would watch the palomino jump gracefully and give the boys a ladylike kick in the muzzle — saving it for the stud.

Out here a week tracking with his six Mimbre riders, former members of the Apache Police at San Carlos, now mustangers working for the Dana Moon Remount & Stage Team Supply Company — if anyone were to ask who he was and what he did.

Though it was not the answer he gave the fool who came riding upwind out of the sun haze. There he was, a speck of sound and smell and the herd was *gone*, like it would run forever, the Mimbres gathering and chasing off through the dust to keep them located. The fool, two black specks now, came clopping across the scrub waste, *clop clop clop clop,* leading a pack animal, not even knowing what a goddamn fool he was.

Yet he appeared to be a rider himself, sweat-dirty Stetson down on his eyes, someone who should know better.

A little bell rang inside Moon's head.

Pay attention.

"Are you Dana Moon?"

An official tone. A policeman verifying the name before saying you're under arrest. Or a messenger boy from somewhere.

"You just wiped out a week of tracking," Moon said. "You know it?"

"I guess it ain't your day," the man said and drew a pistol and immediately began firing at Moon, shooting him in the thigh, just above his right knee, shooting his horse through the neck and withers, the horse screaming and throwing its head as Moon drew his Colt's and shot the man twice through the chest.

He was a fool after all, not as real as he appeared. But who was he?

One of Moon's Mimbre riders, who was called Red, came back to find his boss sitting on the ground twisting his polka-dot scarf around his leg. The leg looked a mess, the entire thigh bleeding where the bullet had dug its way through Moon's flesh to come out just below his hip bone.

"I never even saw him before," Moon said. "See if he's got a wallet or something." He knew the man lying by his horse was dead; he didn't have to ask that.

There were seventeen dollars in a wallet and a folded soiled letter addressed to Asa Maddox, c/o Maricopa Cattle Company, Bisbee, Arizona

58

Territory. The tablet-paper letter said:

Asa Maddox:
That was good news you sent that you have
finally got him located. If you do not want
to wait for us I cannot stop you, but then
we will not wait for you either and will
proceed with our plan to get the other one.
I think you are wrong in doing this alone
instead of with us, but as I have mentioned
I cannot stop you nor do I blame you much
for your eagerness.

Good luck.
(Signed)
J.A. McWilliams

Moon said, "Who is Asa Maddox? Who in
the hell is J. A. McWilliams?"
Red, hunkered down next to Moon, looked at
him but did not say anything.
"Well, shit," Moon said. "I guess I'm going to
Benson a week early."

Florence: May, 1888

The cowboy standing at the end of the Grayback Hotel bar said, "Are you Captain Early?"

From his midpoint position, Bren Early's gaze moved from his glass of cold beer down in that direction.

"I am."

"There is a man here looking for you."

The man who stepped out from behind the rangy cowboy, a large-framed man himself, wore a dark business suit, a gold watch chain across the vest, a gray Stetson that looked like it had just come out of the box.

"Are you Mr. Johnson?" Bren Early asked. It was the name of the party he was supposed to meet here in Florence.

Instead of answering, the man walked over to a Douglas chair against the back wall where a maroon felt traveling bag sat waiting.

Bren Early liked businessmen hunters who were conscientious about the clause "Fee in Advance" and handed it over before they shook hands and said how much they'd been looking forward to this expedition. Raising his cold beer, Bren Early looked up at the clock on the wall between the back-bar mirrors. It was 11:48

in the morning. He liked the idea of putting five hundred dollars in his pocket before noon. He liked the quiet of a morning barroom — the heat and heavy work left outside with Bo Catlett and the light-blue hunting wagon. He'd bring Bo out a glass of beer after.

The cowboy was still sideways to the bar, facing this way. Like making sure he wasn't going to leave. Or so that he'd see the pistol stuck in the cowboy's belt. Why was this cowboy staring at him?

The man in the business suit was bending over his open traveling bag, taking a lot of time. Why wasn't the money on his person?

Bren Early put down his glass of beer. He heard the man in the business suit say, as the man came around, finally, with the pistol:

"This is for Jack McWilliams, you Indin-loving son of a bitch —"

(Though, the bartender testified at the Pinal County Sheriff's Inquest, the gentleman never got to say the last word.)

Bren Early shot the man with a .44 Smith & Wesson, the slug exploding from the barrel, obliterating the word and taking the man cleanly through the brisket . . . shot the cowboy dead through the heart, heard him drop his weapon and fall heavily as he put the Smith on the man in the business suit again, not 100 percent sure about this one.

The man was slumped awkwardly in a pole-axed daze, half-lying-sitting on the maroon travel bag, bewildered, wondering how his plan had suddenly gone to hell, staring up at Bren Early with maybe ten minutes of life remaining in him.

"You rehearsed that, didn't you?" Bren Early said. "I'll bet it sounded good when you said it to a mirror."

Blood seeped out between the man's fingers pressed to his rib cage, trying to hold himself together, breathing and hearing the wound bubble and breathe back at him, sucking air, the man then breathing quicker, harder, to draw air up into his mouth before the wound got it all.

"You should not have begun that speech," Bren Early said. "But a lot of good it does advising you now, huh? . . . Has anybody an idea who this man is?"

J. A. McWilliams of Prescott, a supplier of drilling equipment and high explosives, according to identifying papers. The cowboy with him remained nameless — at least to Bren Early, who left Florence with Bo Catlett and their blue hunting wagon as soon as he was cleared of any willful intent to do harm.

"What's your dad do, whittle and say wise things?"

"He runs a cattle outfit and drives here twice a year," the McKean girl said. "When I got home from Old Mexico he rode up to San Carlos to shoot that one-eyed Apache dead, but they'd already shipped him off to Indian Territory."

"You have a deep fondness and respect for your old dad, haven't you?"

"He's the only one I got and he isn't that old."

"Man that marries you has to measure up to him?"

"I'd be a fool to choose less, wouldn't I?"

"I got to meet this dad of yours," Moon said.

"I'll fetch you in a buckboard," the McKean girl said.

During his third week Moon went downriver to a cluster of adobes, the McKean homestead, and sat out under the ramada in the early evening with her dad. They discussed gunshot wounds, reservation Indians, cattle, graze and wild horses. After a little while McKean invited Moon to share some corn whiskey with little specks of charcoal in it.

"You want to marry my daughter?"

Maybe important decisions were made like

McWilliams. It was a somewhat familiar name, but did not stir any clear recollections from the past.

3

Benson: May, 1888

For nearly a month Dana Moon lived in Room 107 of the Charles Crooker Hotel, waiting for his wound to heal. With the windows facing east it was a hot room mornings, but he liked it because it gave him a view of country and cottonwoods along the river. In the evening he listened to train whistles and the banging-clanging activity over in the switch yard.

He had planned to come to Benson a week later to visit the whorehouse and maybe call on Katy McKean and see if there was a future respectable possibility there.

Now Katy McKean was calling on him. The first time she came he wondered: Will she leave the hotel room door open?

No, she didn't. She sat in the big chair between the windows, and Moon, sitting upright in bed, had to squint to see her face with the sun glare on the windows. He couldn't ask her to pull the shades. After her second visit he got up and struggled one-legged with the horsehide chair, moving it all the way around the bed and after that, when she came, the good view was to the west.

Well, how have you been? . . . Fine . . . I hardly recognize Benson the way it's grown . . . Has it? . . . You live with your folks? . . . Yes, and three young brothers; a place down the river a few miles . . . Bren ever come by to see you? . . . Now and then.

It required three visits from her before he asked, "How come you aren't married with a place of your own?"

"Why aren't you?"

"It hasn't been something I've thought about," Moon said. "Up till now." (Why was he saying this? He had come to town to visit the whorehouse and look at possibilities only.)

"Well, I haven't met the man yet," the McKean girl said. "They come out, my dad looks them over. The best he gives is a shrug. The drag riders he won't even speak to."

"Your dad," Moon said. "Whose choice is it, yours or his?"

"He knows a few things I haven't learned yet," the McKean girl said. She wore boots under her cotton skirt, the toes hooked on the sideboard of Moon's bed, her knees raised and a little apart. He couldn't see anything, but he was aware of her limbs and imagined them being very white and smooth, white thighs — Jesus — and a patch of soft hair.

Moon sat up straight in bed, the comforter pulled up to his waist over his clean longjohns, his hair and mustache combed, bay rum rubbed into his face and wearing his polka-dot scarf loosely for her visit. He was seasoned and weathered for his thirty-four years, looking closer to forty. The McKean girl was about twenty-three, a good-looking woman who could have her pick but was in no hurry; knew her own mind, or her dad's. Bren Early was thirty one or thirty two, closer to her age, liked the ladies and they liked him. Why, Moon wondered, did he always think of Bren when the McKean was here? Hell, ask her.

"Are you interested in Bren?"

"*In*terested? You mean to marry?"

"Yes."

"What's he got to offer? A wagon painted blue to look like a Conestoga, a string of horses . . . What else?"

"I wasn't thinking of what he owns."

"He's full of himself."

"He's got potential."

"Who hasn't?"

"What's your dad think of him?"

"My dad says time's passed him by."

64

65

any other. Without thinking too much. "Yes, I do."

"I don't see what in the hell you got to give her."

"Me," Moon said.

"Well, you present more in person than any I've seen, including General Early; but what does she do, camp with your Mimbres and eat mule?"

"I'll think of a way," Moon said.

The next day when the McKean girl came to visit, and before she could sit down, Moon pulled her to him, felt her hold back till he got her down on the bed, lying across it, felt a terrible pain in his wounded thigh from the exertion and sweat break out on his forehead.

She said, "How're you going to do it?"

He thought she meant perform the act of love. "Don't worry, it can be done."

"You're gonna leave mustanging?"

"Oh," Moon said.

"And settle someplace?"

Moon nodded solemnly and said, "I love you," the first time in his life hearing the actual statement out loud.

"I hope so," the McKean girl said. "We can kiss and you can touch me up here if you want, but that's all till I see what my future is."

"It's a deal," Moon said.

He never did make it to the whorehouse. In fact, he swore he would never visit one again as long as he lived.

4

Apache Pass Station: September, 1888

This trip Bren Early had taken a party from Chicago, three men and the wife of one of them, south of the Pass into the Chiricahua Mountains for mule deer and a look at some authentic Apache Indians. The eastern hunters remained in camp while Bren and Bo Catlett drove the blue wagon to Apache Pass to pick up whiskey and supplies shipped down in the stage from Willcox. Bren was happy to get away from his five-hundred-dollar party.

He was in the back of the wagon, yawning and stretching, waking up from a nap, as Bo Catlett pulled the team into the station yard, Bo yelling at the agent's three kids to get out of the way. There were riding horses in the corral and, on the bench in front of the adobe, three saddles where they usually kept the wash basins. An olla of water hung from the mesquite-pole awning. Going inside, Bo Catlett noticed the saddles.

Three men who looked to have been sleeping as well as traveling in their suits of clothes were playing cards at the near end of the long passenger table. Edgar Watson, the station agent, said, "Where's the Captain?"

Bo Catlett didn't answer him. One of the men at the table stood up and moved to the door to look out. Edgar Watson was at the window now. He said, "There he is."

Looking past the man in the door, Bo Catlett could see Captain Early coming out of the wagon, climbing over the tailgate. The man in the doorway said to Edgar Watson, "Tell your kids to come inside." The other two were also standing now, both holding rifles. A shotgun lay on the table.

Pretending not to notice anything, Bo Catlett said, "Mr. Watson, draw a glass of beer if you will, please."

Edgar Watson, seeming bewildered, said a strange thing, considering what was going on in this close, low-ceilinged room. He said, "You know I can't serve you in here."

Bo Catlett believed he was born in Arkansas or Missouri. He was liberated by Jayhawkers and, at age fifteen, joined the 1st Kansas Colored Volunteers at Camp Jim Lane in February, 1863; saw immediate combat against Rebel

69

irregulars and Missouri bushwhackers and was wounded at Honey Springs in June of '63. He guarded Confederate prisoners at Rock Island; served with the Occupation at Galveston and saw picket duty on the Rio Grande before transferring to the Department of Arizona where he drew the 10th Cavalry, Fort Huachuca, as his last regimental home in a twenty-four-year Army career. Some white officer – before Bren Early's time – dubbed Benjamin Catlett the *beau sabruer* of the nigger outfit and that was how he got his nickname. Bo Catlett was mustered out not long after the Sonora Incident – which did not affect his record – and had been working for Captain Early Hunting Expeditions, Inc. almost a year now. He liked to hear Bren Early talk about the war because the Captain was like a history book, full of information about battles and who did what. It didn't matter the Captain was still a little seven-year old boy when fifteen-year-old Bo Catlett was getting shot through the hip at Honey Springs, or that the Captain didn't get his commission till something like ten years after Appomattox Court House. The Captain knew his war. He told Bo Catlett that he had never objected to colored boys being in the Army or killing white men during the war. But he would admit with candor his disappointment at being assigned to the Colored 10th rather than the "Dandy 5th," George Rosebud Crook's fighting outfit. No, the Captain had nothing against colored people.

There were sure some who did, though.

And there were some who had it in for the Captain, too.

Bren Early, standing by the tailgate of the wagon, wasn't wearing his revolvers. But as soon as he saw the three saddles on the wash bench and heard Edgar Watson call to his kids, Bren reached over the wagon gate, pulled his gunbelt toward him and was in that position, left arm inside, his fingers touching one of his revolvers, when the man's voice said, "We didn't expect you for a couple more days."

Bren looked over his right shoulder at the three coming out from the adobe, two rifles, a shotgun in the middle, and said to himself, Shit. There wasn't any way to mistake their intention.

The man with the shotgun, wearing a hat, an old suit and no collar or tie, said, "I'm R. J. Baker."

Bren Early waited. Yes? Why was that supposed to tell him anything? He said, "How do you do?" seeing Bo Catlett coming out of the adobe behind them: his dear friend and fellow cavalryman, the twenty-four-year seasoned campaigner he hoped to hell was at this moment armed to his teeth.

The man with the shotgun said, "It's time to even a score, you wavy-haired son of a bitch."

Wavy-haired, Bren Early thought and said, "If you intend to try it, you'd better look around behind you."

"God Almighty, you think I'm dumb!" the man named Baker said, as though it was the final insult. He jammed the shotgun to his shoulder; the barrels of the two rifles came up, metal flashing in the afternoon sunlight, and there was no way to stop them.

Edgar Watson, the station agent, had told his wife and children to stay in the kitchen. He heard the gunfire all at once, at least four or five shots exploding almost simultaneously. Edgar Watson rushed to the window by the bar and looked out to see the three cardplayers lying on the hardpack, Bren Early standing out by his wagon with a smoking revolver; then the colored man, Bo, who must have been just outside the house, walking out to look at the three on the ground.

When they came in, Edgar Watson drew a beer and placed it on the bar for Bren Early. He was surprised then when the colored man, Bo, raised an old Navy Colt's — exactly like the one kept under the bar — and laid it on the shiny oak surface. The colored man said, "Thank you for the use," before Edgar Watson realized it *was* his own gun. Bren Early told him to draw a beer for his friend Bo and Edgar Watson did so. Upon examining the Colt's, he found two rounds had been fired from the gun. Still, when Edgar Watson told the story later — and as many times as he told it — it was Bren Early who had shot the three cardplayers when they tried to kill him.

5

McKean's Ranch on the San Pedro: October, 1888

Moon rode up in the cool of early evening leading the palomino on a hackamore. He dropped the rope and the good-looking young mare stood right where she was, not flicking a muscle.

"She reminded me of you," Moon said to the McKean girl, who replied:

"I hope not her hind end."

"Her hair and her eyes," Moon said. "She answers to Goldie."

The McKean girl's mother and dad and three brothers came out to look at the palomino, the

73

horse shying a little as they put their hands on her. Mr. McKean said the horse was still pretty green, huh? Moon said no, it was the horse had not seen so many people before at one time and felt crowded. They kidded him that he was bringing horses now, courting like an Indian.

Moon told them at supper he had been offered a government job as agent at White Tanks, working for the Bureau of Indian Affairs. He would be paid $1,500 a year and given a house and land for farming.

All the McKeans looked at Katy who was across the table from him, the mother saying it sounded wonderful.

Moon did not feel natural sitting there waiting for approval. He said, "But I don't care for flat land, no matter if it has good water and will grow anything you plant. I'm not a grain farmer. I told them I want high graze and would pick my own homesite or else they could keep their wonderful offer."

The McKeans all looked at Katy again.

"They're thinking about it," Moon said. "Meanwhile I got horse contracts to deliver."

"When'll you be back?" Mr. McKean asked.

"Not before Christmas."

"You wait too long," McKean said, "this girl might not be here."

"It's up to me when I get back and up to her

if she wants to wait." Moon felt better as soon as he said it.

6

St. Helen: February, 1889

Bren Early said hadn't they met here one time before? Moon said it was a small world, wasn't it?

Moon here delivering a string of horses to the Hatch & Hodges relay station. Bren Early here to make a stage connection, out of the hunting expedition business and going to Tucson to sleep in a feather bed with a woman and make all the noise he wanted.

He said, "Do you know what it's like to make love to a woman dying for it and have to be quiet as a snake lest you wake up her husband?"

"No, I don't," Moon said, "but I'm willing to hear about it."

There was snow up in the Rincons, a wind moaning outside, a dismal, depressing kind of day. But snug inside the relay station. They stood at the bar and had whiskey before Bren shed his buffalo overcoat and Moon peeled off his sheepskin and wornout chaps. Then sat at

75

the plank table with a bottle of whiskey and mugs of coffee, smelling meat frying; next to them were giant shadows on the plaster wall, dark twin images in a glow of coal-oil light. Like two old pards drinking and catching up on each other's life, wondering how they could have spent a whole year and a half apart. Neither one of them mentioned the McKean girl.

The main topic: Was somebody shooting at you? Yeah — you too? And getting that business finally cleared up. Bren saying he had come out here to be an Indian Fighter and so far had killed nine white men, counting the first two from the bunch in Sonora (the two Bo Catlett had shot), and two he would tell Moon about presently. Moon, not digging up any bodies from the past, said, Well, you're ahead of me there.

But what about this loving a woman and not making any noise?

"Something happens to those women when they come out here," Bren said. "Or it's the type of woman to begin with, likes to put a Winchester to her shoulder and feel it kick."

"Or the wavy-haired guide giving her his U.S. Cavalry look," Moon said. "You wear your saber?"

Bren straightened a little as if to argue, then

76

shrugged, admitting yes, there was a point in that he was a man of this western country; and the woman's husband, out here with his gold-plated Henry in a crocodile case, was still a real-estate man from Chicago or a home builder from Pittsburgh.

"Get to the good part," Moon said.

Bren told him about the party he took up into the Chiricahuas: the man named Bert Grumbach, millionaire president of Prudential Realty in Chicago; his colored valet; a young assistant in Grumbach's company who wore a stiff collar and necktie, as the man did; and the man's wife Greta, yes indeed, who was even rounder and better-looking than that French actress Sarah Bernhardt.

As soon as he met them at Willcox with the wagon and saddle horses, Bren said he could see what kind of trip it was going to be: the man, Bert Grumbach, one of those know-it-all talkers, who'd been everywhere hunting and had a game room full of trophies to prove it, considered this trip not much more than going out back to shoot rabbits. The wife, Greta, was quiet, not at all critical like other wives. ("How many times you gonna tell that tiger story?" Or, "You think drinking all that whiskey proves you're a man?") No, Bert Grumbach would be talking away and Bren would feel Greta's eyes

77

on him. He'd glance over and sure enough, she'd be staring, giving him a calm, steady look with her eyes. Christ, Bren said, you knew exactly what she wanted.

She did not try to outdo her husband either, though she was a fair shot for a woman, dropping a mule-deer buck at two hundred yards with a clean hit through the shoulders.

Moon asked if they left deer laying all over the mountain and Bren said no, the guides took most of the meat to the fort Indians at Bowie.

It wasn't all hunting. Time was spent sitting around camp drinking, eating venison steaks, talking and drinking some more, Grumbach belittling the setup and the fare. Bren said he would perform a routine with his .44 Russians, blowing up a row of dead whiskey bottles, which the Eastern hunters usually ate up. Except Grumbach wasn't impressed. He had a matched pair of Merwin & Hulbert six-shooters, beauties he took out of a rosewood box, nickle-plated with carved ivory grips. He'd aim, left hand on his hip, and fire and hit bottles, cans, pine cones at twenty paces, chipmunks, ground squirrels, ospreys and horned owls. He was a regular killer, Bren said.

"And he caught you with his wife," Moon said.

"Not outright," Bren said. "I believe he only

78

suspected, but it was enough."

What happened, Greta began coming to Bren's tent late at night. The first time, he tried in a nice way to get her to leave; but as she took her robe off and stood bare-ass, she said unless he did likewise she would scream. There was no choice but to give in to her, Bren said. But it was ticklish business, her moaning and him saying shhh, be quiet, his nerves alive as another part of him did the job at hand. Five or six nights, that was the drill.

The morning of the final day of the hunt, Bert Grumbach walked up to Bren, slapped his face with a glove and said, "I assume you will choose pistols. May I suggest twenty paces?"

Moon had an idea what happened next, since Bren was sitting here telling it; but he did not interrupt or even pick up his whiskey glass as Bren continued.

Bren said to the man, Now wait a minute. You know what you're doing? The man said he demanded satisfaction, his honor being abused. Bren said, But is it worth it? You might die. Grumbach gave him a superior look and had his assistant draw up a paper stating this was a duel of honor and if one of the participants was killed or injured, the other would not be legally culpable, hereby and so on, attesting with their signatures they were entering into it willingly

79

and pledging to exonerate the other of blame whatever the outcome.

Bren said they stood about sixty feet apart, each with a revolver held at his side. Bo Catlett would fire his own weapon, the assistant holding a rifle on Bo to see he fired up in the air, and that would be the signal.

"Yeah?" Moon said, hunching over the plank table.

"Aiming at a man and seeing him drawing a bead on you isn't the same as shooting chipmunks," Bren said, "or even wilder animals."

"No, it isn't," Moon said. "He hurried, didn't he?"

"He dropped his hand from his off hip, stood straddle-legged and began firing as fast as he could. Having to protect myself, I shot him once, dead center."

"What did Greta do?"

"Nothing. We rolled Grumbach up in a piece of canvas, had a coffin made in Willcox and shipped him home with his legal papers. Greta said thank you very much for a wonderful and exciting time."

"Well," Moon said, "you have come to be a shooter, haven't you?"

"Not by choice," Bren said. "There was another fella at Bowie tried his luck when I sold my wagon and string. Announced he was an

80

old compadre of one Clement Hurd. How come they all tracked after me and only one of them tried for you as a prize?"

"You advertise," Moon said. "Captain Early, the great hunter and lover. When did you get promoted?"

"I thought it sounded like a proper rank to have," Bren said. "Well, I've bid farewell to the world of commerce and won't be advertising any more. It's a good business if you have an agreeable nature and can stand grinning at people who don't know hotcakes from horse-shit."

"I'm leaving my business, too," Moon said. "Gonna try working for the government one more time."

Bren Early was off somewhere in his mind. He sighed, turning in his chair to sit back against his shadow on the plaster wall.

"Down in Sonora that time, we stood at the line, didn't we?"

"We stood at the line," Moon said.

"I guess it's something you make up your mind to," Bren Early said, "if you don't care to kiss ass. But my, it can complicate your life."

Chapter V

Young Maurice Dumas of the *Chicago Times* looked at his list of THINGS TO DO:

Interview W.A. Vandozen, LaSalle Mining v.p. staying at Congress.

How? The only chance would be to run into the man accidentally, as he did with Early, and show the man he was courteous (took his cap off), industrious and did not ask personal or embarrassing questions or make brash assumptions.

And then kiss his hinie, why don't you? Maurice Dumas thought.

It had been pure luck with Brendan Early, the timing, catching him in a talkative mood. Then being invited out to the desert to watch him shoot: amazing, studying the man as he calmly blazed away with two different sets of matched revolvers: one pair, Smith & Wesson, big and mean-looking; the other, ivory-handled, nickle-plated Merwin & Hulberts that Early said were given to him by a wealthy and grateful lady from Chicago. Not saying why she had been grateful. At first — out there shooting at saguara and barrel cactus that were about the girth of a man — Early seemed trouble about the accuracy of his weapons. But within an hour his confidence was restored and as they rode back to Sweetmary Early told about the Sonora Incident and what he knew of Phil Sundeen. Which covered the next item on Maurice Dumas' THINGS TO DO.

Find out about this Sundeen.

Early said he had assumed the man was buried beneath Mexican soil and was surprised to learn he was alive and kicking. Different other LaSalle Mining people said that Sundeen had been hired by the company as Supervisor in Charge of Protection and Public Safety and was to see that no one infringed on company leases, destroyed company property or exposed themselves to harm or injury in areas related to company mining operations.

What?

The news reporters in the Gold Dollar said what it meant in plain English: Phil Sundeen had been hired to bust heads, shoot trespassers and run them off company land. And that included all the Indians, niggers and Mexicans living up in the Rincons. For months the two sides had been threatening and calling each other names. Finally, as soon as Sundeen arrived, there would be some action to write about. Yes, the company had called him in, a spokesman said, as an expert in restoring order and maintaining peace.

Good, the newsmen said, because it certainly wasn't much of a war without any shooting.

"I said restore peace," the company spokesman said. And a reporter said, "We know what you mean."

But wait a minute. Why hire Sundeen? Why not let Bren Early, known to be a shooter, restore order and maintain peace?

Because Mr. Early had his own responsibilities as Coordinating Manager of the Southwest Region, the company spokesman said.

According to the journalists that was a pile of horse shit. Not one of them, including Maurice Dumas, had yet to see Bren Early sitting at a desk or coordinating much other than a draw poker hand. Bren Early had been hired as part of the deal when the company bought his claims, and his executive title had been made up out of thin air. They *could* put him to work if they wanted. Otherwise Early was to keep himself available to show visiting dignitaries and politicians the Works: which meant the local whorehouses and gambling parlors and — if the visitors were inclined — take them out hunting or to look at some live Indians. It was said the company was paying Early a guaranteed $100,000 over ten years, plus a one-percent royalty on all the milled copper sent to market. He was a rich man.

O.K., but now Early and Sundeen were on the same side. What about the bitterness between them — as reported by Maurice Dumas? How would it affect the Early-Moon Feud? Would it be like a preliminary event, winner getting to go against Dana Moon?

The journalists sat down to have a few drinks and think about that one, see if they could develop a side issue cross-plot to lay over the main action. They fooled with possible headline themes such as:

Prospect of Preliminary Showdown Delays War
Will New Man Live to Take Command?
Shoot-out Expected on LaSalle Street.

All this even before Phil Sundeen arrived in town. If he had the least intention of gunning for Bren Early he would find the atmosphere most conducive.

Meanwhile, Maurice Dumas was working on the third item on his list of THINGS TO DO.

Interview Dana Moon.

When Maurice Dumas arrived at White Tanks he didn't know what was going on: all these Apaches, about a hundred of them out in the pasture near the agency buildings and stock pens, sitting around campfires, roasting chunks of beef while others were chanting and a line of women were doing some kind of shuffle dance. Like it was an Indian Fourth of July picnic or some kind of tribal pow-pow. Some of the men wore hats and parts of white men's clothes, a pair of trousers, a vest; though most of them still wore skirts and high moccasins and thick headbands wrapped around their coarse hair.

Maurice Dumas found out it was Meat Day. When the beef allotment provided by the government was delivered, the Apaches always butchered a few head on the spot and had a feast. They would stuff themselves with meat, eating it straight, drink some corn beer, or tulapai, as it was called, spend the night here in the agency pasture and, in the morning, drive their skimpy herd up into the mountains to their rancherías. Maurice Dumas remembered being told that Apaches always camped high and wouldn't be caught dead living down in the flats. It was part of the problem in this land dispute which he wanted to discuss with Dana Moon — if he could find him.

Well, it seemed he was getting luckier all the time — just by chance arriving on Meat Day — dismounting his hired horse in front of the Indian Agency office, a one-story adobe building with a wooden front porch, and there was Moon himself sitting in a straight chair tilted back, his boots up on the porch rail, at rest. Perfect, Maurice Dumas thought. The Indian agent in his seat of governmental authority, while his charges performed their tribal rites.

Moon looked exactly as he did in the C. S. Fly photos, though not as buttoned up and strapped together. He did not appear to be armed. His belt buckle was undone and he was smoking a cigar. When Maurice Dumas introduced himself, Moon asked if he would like something to eat. The news reporter said no thanks. He handed Moon a paper bag saying, "A little something for you," and watched as Moon took out the bottle of Green River bourbon whiskey and read the label unhurriedly before placing the quart on the plank floor next to him. "Thank you," he said.

"I just wanted to talk to you a little," Maurice Dumas said. "Ask your opinion of a few things."

"Ask," Moon said.

"I didn't think you lived here at the agency."

"I don't. I'm a few miles up that barranca," lowering his head and looking west, beyond the pasture and the gathering of feasting Indians. "I'm here for Meat Day and will leave soon as I'm able to." He seemed full but not too uncomfortable.

"Do you live up there alone?"

"My wife and I."

"Oh, I didn't know you were married."

"Why would you?"

"I mean nobody's mentioned it."

"Does it make a difference in how you see me?"

"I mean I'm just surprised," Maurice Dumas said. "If there's gonna be trouble and all — I was thinking, having your wife there could make it harder for you."

Moon said, "Do you know how many wives are up there? How many families?"

"I guess I hadn't thought of it."

"You call it a war, you like to keep it simple," Moon said. "These men against those men. Line 'em up, let's see who wins. Well, to do that we'd have to get rid of the women and children. Where should we send them?"

"As I said, I hadn't thought about it."

"What do you think about?" Moon asked.

The front legs of the chair hit the plank floor as Moon got up and went into the agency office.

Now what? Was he offended by something? No, Moon came out again with two glasses, sat down and poured them a couple of drinks.

Maurice Dumas pulled a chair over next to Moon's. "I'm only an observer," he said, sitting down and carefully tilting back. "I don't take sides, I remain objective."

"You're on a side whether you like it or not," Moon said. "You're on the side of commerce and, I imagine, you believe in progress and good government."

"What's wrong with that?"

"Copper is progress and the land has been leased to the mine company by the government."

Maurice Dumas didn't like the insinuation. "That doesn't mean I'm on the side of the company. But if we're talking about legal rights, I'd have to say *they*, the legal right, are. The company owns mineral rights to the land for a hundred years."

"You feel that's long enough?"

"I don't know how long it takes."

Moon took a sip of whiskey and drew on his cigar. "You happen to know what the mine company's doing up there?"

"Right now they're surveying," Maurice Dumas said, "trying to locate veins and ore loads that look promising."

"And how are they doing that?"

"As I understand, they set off dynamite, then pick around, see what they've got."

Moon waited.

"So far, I guess they haven't found anything worth sinking a shaft in."

"But they spook the herds, scatter 'em all over, kill what they want for meat," Moon said. "They've blown up stock tanks, ruined the natural watershed, wiped out crops and some homes in rock slides. They tear up a man's land, clean him out, and leave it."

"It's theirs to tear up," the news reporter said.

"No, it isn't," Moon said, in a quiet but ominous tone.

The whiskey made Maurice Dumas feel confident and knowledgeable. He said, "I'd like to say you're right. Good for you. But the fact remains your Indians are off the White Tanks reservation by several miles. And the other people up there, whoever they are, are living on land without deed or title. So LaSalle Mining, legally, has every right to make them leave."

"You asked my opinion," Moon said. "Are you gonna print it in the paper?"

"I hope to, yes."

"You're not writing anything down."

"I have a good memory," Maurice Dumas said.

"Well, remember this," Moon said. "The Mimbre Apaches were hunting up there before Christopher Columbus came over in his boat, and till now nobody's said a word about it, not even the Indian Bureau. There's a settlement of colored people, colored soldiers who've taken Indian wives, all of them at one time in the United States Tenth Cavalry. You would think the government owed them at least a friendly nod, wouldn't you? The Mexicans living up there have claims that go back a hundred years or more to Spanish land grants. The Mexicans went to Federal Claims Court to try to protect their property. They got thrown out. I wrote to the Indian Bureau about the Apaches up there — it's *their* land, let 'em live on it. No, they said, get your people back to White Tanks or you're fired. You see the influence the company has? Generations they've hunted, roamed through those mountains. Government doesn't say a word till the big company kneels on 'em for a favor. Yes sir, we'll see to it right away, Mr. LaSalle —"

"Is there a Mr. LaSalle?" Maurice didn't think so.

"I went to Federal District Court to get an

91

injunction. I wanted to restrict the mine company to certain areas — they find ore, O.K., they pay a royalty on it to any people that have to move. They don't find any ore, they clean up their mess and get out. The judge held up my injunction — cost me fifty dollars to have written — like it was paper you keep in the privy and threw it out of court."

"Legal affairs get complicated," the news reporter offered.

"Do you want to tell me how it is," Moon said, "or you want to listen."

"I'm sorry. Go on."

"All these people I've mentioned number only about two hundred and sixty, counting old ones, women and young children. Fewer than fifty able-bodied men. And they're spread all over. By that, I mean they don't present any kind of unified force. The mine company can send a pack of armed men up there with guns and dynamite to take the land, and you know what will happen?"

"Well, eventually —" the reporter began.

"Before eventually," Moon said. "You know what will happen? Do you want to go ask the people what they'll do if armed men come?"

"Will they tell me?"

"They'll tell you it's their land. If the

92

company wants it, the company will have to take it."

"Well," the news reporter said, a little surprised, "that's exactly what the company will do, take it."

"When you write your article for the paper," Moon said, "don't write the end till it happens."

Chapter VI

1

White Tanks: May, 1889

Moon and four Mimbre Apaches were white-washing the agency office when the McKean girl rode up on her palomino. They appeared to have the job almost done — the adobe walls clean and shining white — and were now slapping the wash on a front porch made of new lumber that looked to be a recent addition.

The McKean girl wore a blue bandana over her hair and a blue skirt that was bunched in front of her on the saddle and hung down on the sides just past the top of her boots.

Sitting her horse, watching, she thought of India: pictures she had seen of whitewashed mud buildings on barren land and little brown men in white breechclouts and turbans —

94

though the headpieces the Apaches wore were rusty red or brown, dark colors, and their black hair hung in strands past their shoulders. It was strange she thought of India Indians and not American Indians. Or not so strange, because this place did not seem to belong in the mountains of Arizona. Other times looking at Apaches, when she saw them close, she thought of gypsies: dark men wearing regular clothes, but in strange, colorful combinations of shirts made from dresses beneath checkered vests, striped pants tucked into high moccasins and wearing jewelry, men wearing beads and metal trinkets. The Mexicans called them barbarians. People the McKean girl knew called them red niggers and heathens.

Moon — he was saying something in a strange tongue and the Apaches, with whitewash smeared over their bare skin, were laughing. She had never heard an Apache laugh, nor had even thought of them laughing before this. Coming here was like visiting a strange land.

One of the Apaches saw her and said something to Moon. He turned from his painting and came down from the porch as the Apaches watched. He looked strange himself: suspenders over his bare, hairy chest, his body pure white but his forearms weathered brown,

like he was wearing long gloves. He was looking at her leg, her thigh beneath the skirt, as he
approached.

She expected him to pat the mare and
pretend to be interested in her, saying how's
Goldie. But he didn't. He looked from her leg
up to her face, squinting in the sun, and said,
"You getting anxious?"

"It's been seven months," Katy McKean said.
"If you've changed your mind I want to know."

"I've been building our house," Moon said.

The McKean girl looked at the whitewashed
adobe, and the stock pens, the outpost on the
barren flats, dressed with a flagpole flying
the stars and stripes. Like a model post office.

"That?" she said.

"Christ, no," Moon said. "That's not a house,
that's a symbol. Our house is seven miles up
the draw, made of 'dobe plaster and stone.
Front porch is finished and a mud fence is
being put up now."

"You like front porches," the McKean girl
said. "Well, they must've given you what you
wanted. What do you do in return?"

"Keep the peace. Count heads. I'm a high-
paid tally hand is what I am."

"Tell them jokes, like you were doing?"

"See eye to eye," Moon said. "A man catches
his wife in the bushes with some other fella —

96

you know what he does? He cuts the end of her nose off. The wife's mother gets upset and tells the police to arrest the husband and punish him and the police dump it in my lap."

"And what do you do?"

"Tell the woman she looks better with a short nose — I don't know what I do," Moon said. "I live near them — not with them — and try not to change their customs too much."

"Like moving to a strange heathen land," the McKean girl said, unconsciously touching her nose.

"Well, Christian people, they caught a woman in adultery they used to stone her to death. Customs change in time."

"But they never do anything to the man," the McKean girl said.

"Ask your dad, the old philosopher, about that one," Moon said. "Ask him if it's all right for you to come live among the heathens."

"When?"

"Next fall sometime," Moon said. "October."

"Next month," the McKean girl said, "the third Saturday in June at St. John the Apostle's, ten A.M. Who's gonna be your best man, one of these little dark fellas?"

The wedding took place the fourth Saturday in June and the best man was Brendan Early:

Bren looking at the bride in church, looking at her in the dining room of the Charles Crooker Hotel where the reception was held, still not believing she had chosen quiet Dana Moon. It wasn't that Bren had sought her hand and been rejected. He had not gotten around to asking her; though it had always been in the back of his mind he might easily marry her someday. Right now, as Dana's wife, she was the best-looking girl he had ever seen, and the cleanest-looking, dressed in white with her blonde hair showing. And now it was too late. Amazing. Like he'd blinked his eyes and two years had passed. They asked him what he was doing these days and he said, well (not about to tell these industrious people he was making a living as a mine-camp cardplayer), he was looking into a mining deal at the present time — saying it because he had in his pocket the title to a staked-out claim he'd won in a $2,000-call poker game. Yes, he was in mining now.

And told others on the Helvetia stage — pushed by a nagging conscience or some curious urge, having seen his old chum settling down with a wife he thought *he* would someday have. Time was passing him by and it wasn't the ticket for a gentleman graduate of the U.S. Military Academy to be making a living dealing faro or peeking at hole cards. Why *not* look into this claim he now owned? He had title and a signed assay report that indicated a pocket of high-yield gold ore if not a lode.

Starting out on that return trip to nowhere he was in mining. Before the stage had reached its destination Bren Early was in an altogether different situation.

2

The Benson-Helvetia Stage: June, 1889

Three very plain-looking ladies who had got off the train from an Eastern trip had so much baggage, inside and out, there was only room for Bren Early and one other passenger; a fifty-year-old dandy who wore a cavalry mustache, his hat brim curved up on one side, and carried a cane with a silver knob.

Bren Early and the Dandy sat next to each other facing the plain-looking, chattering ladies who seemed excitable and nervous and were probably sweating to death in their buttoned-up velvet travel outfits. Facing them wasn't so bad; Bren could look out the window at the countryside moving past in the rickety, rattling pounding of the stagecoach; but the Dandy, with his leather hatbox and travel bag, lounged in a way that took up more than half the seat, sticking his leg out at an angle and forcing Bren Early to sit against the sideboards. Bren nudged the Dandy's leg to acquire more room and the Dandy said, "If you don't mind, sir," sticking his leg out again.

"I do," Bren Early said, "since I paid for half this bench."

"And I paid in receiving a wound to this leg in the war," the Dandy said. "So, if you don't mind."

The ladies gave him sympathetic looks and one of them arranged her travel case so the Dandy could prop his leg on it. The Dandy had a cane, yes, but Bren Early had seen the man walk out of the Benson station to the coach without a limp or faltering gait. Then one of the ladies asked him whom he had served with.

The Dandy said, "I had the honor of serving with the Texas Brigade, Madam, attached to General Longstreet's command, and received my wound at the Battle of the Wilderness, May 6, 1864. Exactly twenty-five years ago last month."

Bren Early listened, thinking, Ask him a question, he gives you plenty of answer. One of the ladies said it must have been horrible being wounded in battle and said she was so thankful she was a woman.

"It was ill fate," the Dandy said, "to be wounded in victory while giving the enemy cold steel, routing them, putting to flight some of the most highly regarded regiments in Yankeedom. But I have no regrets. The fortunes of war sent a minié ball through my leg and an Army wagon delivered me to the hospital at Belle Plain."

"Whose wagon?" Bren Early said.

The Dandy gave him a superior look and said, "Sir?"

"You are only half right in what you tell these ladies," Bren Early said. "You did meet six of the most respected regiments in the Union Army: the Second, Sixth and Seventh Wisconsin, the Nineteenth Indiana and the Twenty-fourth Michigan. You met the men of the Iron Brigade and if you ever meet one again, take off your hat and buy him a drink, for you're lucky to be alive."

"You couldn't have been there," the Dandy said, still with a superior look.

"No," Bren Early said, "but I've studied the action up and down the Orange Plank Road and through the woods set afire by artillery. The Iron Brigade, outnumbered, fought Longstreet to a standstill and *you*, if you were taken to Belle Plain then you went as a prisoner

101

because the Confederate line never reached that far east."

The Dandy looked at the ladies and shrugged with a weary sigh. See what a wounded veteran has to put up with?

Bren Early had to hold on from grabbing the mincing son of a bitch and throwing him out the window. With the ladies giving him cold-fish looks he pulled his new Stetson down over his eyes and made up his mind to sleep.

Lulled by the rumbling racket of the coach he saw himself high on a shelf of rock against a glorious blue sky, a gentle breeze blowing. There he was on the narrow ledge, ignoring the thousand-foot drop directly behind him, swinging his pick effortlessly, dislodging a tremendous boulder and seeing in the exposed seam the glitter of gold particles imbedded in rock, chunks of gold he flicked out with his penknife, nuggets he scooped up from the ground and dropped into canvas sacks. He saw a pile of sacks in a cavern and saw himself hefting them, estimating the weight of his fortune at $35 an ounce . . . $560 a pound . . . $56,000 a hundred pounds . . . He slept and awoke to feel the coach swaying, slowing down, coming to a stop, the three ladies and the Dandy leaning over to look out the windows. The driver, or somebody up above them, was saying, "Everybody do what they say. Don't anybody try to be brave."

The ladies were now even more excitable and nervous and began to make sounds like they were going to cry. The Dandy gathered his hatbox and travel bag against him and slipped his right hand inside his waistcoat.

The voice up top said, "We're not carrying no mail or anything but baggage."

And another voice said, "Let's see if you can step off the boot with your hands in the air."

Shit, Bren Early thought.

His revolvers were in his war-bag beneath his feet, stowed away so as not to upset the homely, twittery ladies, and, for the sake of comfort. What would anybody hope to get robbing this chicken coop? The only important stop between Benson and points west was Sweetmary, a mining town; and he doubted a tacky outfit like this stage line would be entrusted to deliver a payroll. No – he was sure of it, because there was just the driver on top, no armed guard with him, not even a helper. Cheap goddamn outfit.

A rider on a sorrel came up to the side of the coach, Bren seeing his pistol extended, a young cowboy face beneath an old curled-brim hat.

"You, mister," the young rider said to the Dandy, "let me see your paws. All of you keep your paws out in plain sight."

Another one, Bren Early was thinking. Practiced it and it sounded good. Times must be bad.

Looking past the sorrel Bren could see two more riders beyond the road in the scrub, and the driver standing by the front wheel now, a shotgun on the ground. The rider on the sorrel was squinting up at the baggage, nudging his horse closer. He dismounted then and opened the coach door to look in at the petrified ladies in velvet and the two gentlemen across from them. Someone behind the young rider yelled, "Pull that gear offa there!"

Making him do all the work while they sit back, Bren thought. Dumb kid. In bad company.

The young rider stepped up on the rung and into the door opening, reaching up to the baggage rack with both hands. His leather chaps, his gunbelt, his skinny trunk in a dirty cotton shirt were right there, filling the doorway. Bren thinking, He's too dumb to live long at his trade. Hoping the kid wasn't excitable. Let him get out of here with some of the ladies' trinkets and the Dandy's silver cane and think he's made a haul. Bren had three twenty-dollar gold pieces and some change he'd contribute to the cause. Get it done so they could get on with the ride.

Sitting back resigned, letting it happen, Bren wasn't prepared – he couldn't believe it – when the fifty-year-old Dandy made his move, hunching forward as he drew a nickel-plated pistol from inside his coat and shoved the gun at the exposed shirtfront in the doorway, pointing the barrel right where the young rider's shirttail was coming out of his pants as he reached above him.

Bren said, "No!" grabbing at the Dandy's left arm, the man wrenching away and coming back to swat him across the face with his silver-tipped cane – the son of a bitch, if that was the way he wanted it . . . Bren cocked his forearm and backhanded his fist and arm across the man's upper body. But too late. The nickel-plate jabbed into the shirtfront and went off with a report that rang loud in the wooden coach. The young rider cried out, hands in the air, and was gone. The women were screaming now and the Dandy was firing again – the little dude son of a bitch, maybe he *had* raised hell at the Wilderness with his Texas Brigade. He was raising hell now, snapping shots at the two riders until Bren Early backhanded him again, hard, giving himself room to get out of the coach.

He saw the young rider lying on the ground, the sorrel skitting away. He saw the driver kneeling, raising the shotgun and the two mounted men whipping their horses out of there with the twin sounds of the double-barrel reports, the riders streaking dust across the scrub waste, gone, leaving the young rider behind.

Kneeling over him, Bren knew the boy was dead before he touched his throat for a pulse. Dead in an old blood-stained shirt hanging out of his belt; converted Navy cap-and-ball lying in the dust next to him. Poor dumb kid, gone before he could learn anything. He heard the Dandy saying something.

"He's one of them."

Bren Early looked up, seeing the driver coming over, reloading the shotgun.

"I had a feeling about him and, goddamn it, I was right," the Dandy said. "He's the inside man. Tried to stop me."

Bren said, "You idiot. You killed this boy for no reason."

The driver was pointing his shotgun at him, saying, "Put your hands in the air."

Sweetmary: June, 1889

Mr. and Mrs. Dana Moon got out of the
Charles Crooker Hotel in Benson after two
honeymoon nights in the bridal suite and coming down to breakfast to feel everybody in the
dining room looking at them and the waitress
grinning and saying, "Well, how are we this
morning, just fine?" They loaded a buckboard
with their gear, saddles, two trunks of linen,
china and household goods, and took the old
stage road west, trailing their horses. Why stay
cooped up in somebody else's room when they
had a new home in the mountains with an
inside water pump and a view of practically the
entire San Pedro Valley?

In late afternoon they came to Sweetmary, a
town named for a copper mine, a town growing
out of the mine works and crushing mill high
up on the grade: the town beginning from
company buildings and reaching down to flat-
land to form streets, rows of houses and business establishments — Moon remembering it as
a settlement of tents and huts, shebangs made
of scrap lumber, only a year before — the town
growing out of the mine just as the hump
ridges of ore tailings came down the grade from

the mine shafts. LaSalle was the main street and the good hotel was the Congress. One more night in somebody else's bed. In the morning they'd buy a few provisions at the company store and head due north for home.

During this trip Moon said to his wife, "You're a Katy a lot of ways; I think you'll always look young. But you're not a bashful girl, are you? I think you're more of a Kate than a Katy, and that's meant as a compliment."

In the morning, lying in the Congress Hotel bed with the sun hot on the windows, he said, "I thought people only did it at night. I mean married people."

"Who says you have to wait till dark?" She grinned at him and said then, "You mean if you're not married you can do it any time?"

"You do it when you see the chance. I guess that's it," Moon said. "Married people are busy all day, so it's become the custom to do it at night."

"Custom," Kate said. "What's the custom among the Indians? I bet whenever they feel the urge, right? You ever do it outside?"

Moon pretended he had to think to recall and Kate said, "I want to do it outside when we get home."

"I built us a *bed*."

"We'll use the bed. But I want to do it

108

different places. Try different other ways."

Moon looked at this girl lying next to him, amazed. "What other way is there?"

"I don't know if we can do them in the daylight, but I got some ideas." She smiled at him and said, "Being married is fun, you know it?"

Moon was getting dressed, buttoning his shirt, and looking out the window, when he saw Brendan Early. He said, "Jesus Christ." Kate came over in her bloomers to look too.

There he was, Moon's best man, walking along the street in a file of jail prisoners carrying shovels and picks, the group dressed in washed-out denim uniforms — the letter "P" stenciled in white on the shirts and pants — being herded along by several armed men on horseback.

"Jesus Christ," Moon said again, with awe. "What's he done now?"

When Moon found them, the work detail was clearing a drainage ditch about two miles from town, up in the hills back of the mine works. Mounted, he circled and came down from above them to approach Bren Early working with a shovel, in his jail uniform, his new Stetson dirty and sweat-stained. There were four guards with shotguns. The one on the high side, dismounted and sitting about ten yards off in the shade of a cedar stand, heard Moon first and raised his shotgun as he got to his feet.

"Don't come no closer!"

Now Bren Early straightened and was looking this way, leaning on the high end of his shovel. He watched Moon nudging his buckskin down toward them — not knowing Moon's game, so not calling out or saying anything.

"I said don't come no closer!"

This man with the shotgun was the Cochise County Deputy Sheriff for Sweetmary. His name — Moon had learned in town — was R.J. Bruckner. Moon said it now, inquiringly.

"Mr. Bruckner?"

"What do you want?"

There did not appear to be any warmth or cordiality in the man. He was heavy-set and mean-looking with a big nose and a florid complexion to go with his ugly disposition. Moon would try sounding patient and respectful and see what happened.

He said, "My, it's a hot day to be working, isn't it?"

"You got business with me, state it," Bruckner said, "or else get your nosey ass out of here."

My oh my, Moon thought, taking off his hat

110

and resetting it low against the sun, giving himself a little time to adjust and remain calm. The plug of tobacco in his jaw felt dry and he sucked on it a little.

"I wonder if I could have a word with one of your prisoners."

"God Almighty," Bruckner said, "get the hell away from here."

"That good-looking fella there, name of Early. His mama's worried about him," Moon said, "and sent me out looking."

"Tell his mama she can visit him at Yuma. That boy's going away for twenty years."

"Can I ask what he's done?"

"Held up the Benson stage and was caught at it."

Bren Early, standing in the drainage ditch, was shaking his head slowly, meaning no, he didn't, or just weary of it all.

"Has he been tried already?"

"Hasn't come up yet."

"Then how do you know he's getting twenty years?"

"It's what I'll recommend to the Circuit Court in Tombstone."

"Oh," Moon nodded, showing how agreeable he was. "When is the trial going to be?"

"When I take him down there," Bruckner said.

"Pretty soon now?"

"When I decide," Brunckner said, irritated now. "Get the hell away from here 'fore I put you in the ditch with him."

R.J. Bruckner did not know at that moment – as Moon's hand went to his shirtfront but stopped before going inside the coat – how close he was to being shot.

Back at the Congress Hotel Moon said to his wife, "I have never had the urge like I did right then. It's not good, to be armed and feel like that."

"But understandable," Kate said. "What are we gonna do?"

"Stay here another night, if it's all right."

"Whatever you decide," his wife said. She loved this man very much, but sometimes his calmness frightened her. She watched him wash and change his shirt and slip on the shoulder holster that held the big Colt's revolver – hidden once his coat was on, but she knew it was there and she knew the man, seeing him again standing at the adobe wall in Sonora.

After supper Mr. and Mrs. Moon sat in rocking chairs on the porch of the Congress Hotel – Kate saying, "This is what you like to do, huh?" – until the Mexican boy came up to them and said in Spanish, "He left." Moon gave the boy two bits and walked down LaSalle Street to the building with the sign that said DEPUTY SHERIFF – COCHISE COUNTY.

Inside the office he told the assistant deputy on duty he was here to see a prisoner, one Brendan Early and, before the deputy could say anything, laid a five-dollar piece on the man's desk.

"Open your coat," the deputy said.

Moon handed the man his Colt's, then followed him through a locked door, down an aisle of cells and up a back stairway to a row of cells on the second floor. Moon had never seen a jail this size, able to hold thirty or more prisoners, in a dinky mining town.

"You know *why*," Bren Early said, talking to Moon through the bars – the deputy standing back a few paces watching them – "because the son of a bitch is making money off us. The mine company pays him fifty cents a day per man to work on roads and drainage and this horse fart Bruckner puts it in his pocket."

"You talk to a lawyer?"

"Shit no, not till I go to trial. Listen, there's rummies in here for drunk and disorderly been working *months*. He thinks I'm a road agent, I could be in here a *year* before I ever see a courtroom. And then I got to face this other idiot who's gonna point to me and say I tried to rob the stage."

"Did you?"

"Jesus Christ, I'm telling you, I don't get out of here I'm gonna take my shovel and bust it over that horse fart's head."

"You're looking pretty good though," Moon said. "Better'n you did at the wedding trying to drink up all the whiskey."

Close to the bars Bren Early said, "You gonna get me out of here or I have to do it myself?"

"I have to take my wife home," Moon said. "Then, after that."

"After that, what? I'm not gonna last any time in this place. You know it, too."

"Don't get him mad at you," Moon said. "Say please and thank you or else keep your mouth shut till I get back."

"When — goddamn it."

"You might see it coming," Moon said, "but I doubt it."

This jail was hard time with no relief. Chop rocks and clear ditches or sweat to death in that second-floor, tin-roof cell. (The Fourth of July they sat up there listening to fools shooting their guns off in the street, expecting any moment bullets to come flying in the barred windows.) Bren Early could think of reports

114

he'd read describing Confederate prisons, like Belle Isle in the James River and Libby's warehouse in Richmond, where Union soldiers rotted away and died by the thousands. Compared to those places the Sweetmary lockup was a resort hotel. But Bren would put R.J. Bruckner up with any of the sadistic guards he'd read about, including the infamous Captain Wirz of Andersonville.

One day after work Bruckner marched Bren Early down to the basement of the jail and took him into a room that was like a root cellar. Bren hoped for a moment he would be alone with Bruckner, but two other deputies stood by with pick handles while Bruckner questioned him about the stage holdup.

"One of your accomplices, now deceased, was named Pierson. What are the names of the other two?"

They stood with the lantern hanging behind them by the locked door.

"I wasn't part of it, so I don't know," Bren Early said.

Bruckner stepped forward and hooked a fist into Bren's stomach and Bren hit him hard in the face, jolting him; but that was his only punch before the two deputies stepped in, swinging their pick handles, and beat him to the dirt floor.

Bruckner said, "What's the names of your other two chums?"

Bren said, "I never saw 'em before."

"Once more," Bruckner said.

"I'll tell you one thing," Bren said.

"What is that?"

"When I get out I'm gonna tear your nose off, you ugly shit-face son of a bitch."

As with J.A. McWilliams, killed in Florence a year before while calling Bren Early some other kind of son of a bitch, did he say it all or not? Bren did not quite finish before Bruckner hit him with his fists and the deputies waded in to beat him senseless with the pick handles. Dumb, wavy-haired know-it-all; they fixed him. And they'd see he never let up a minute out on the work detail . . . where Bren would look up at the high crests and at the brushy ravines and pray for Moon to appear as his redeemer.

"You might see it coming, but I doubt it," Moon had said.

Moon brought six Mimbre Apaches with him: the one named Red and five other stalkers who had chased wild horses with him, had served on the Apache Police at San Carlos and had raised plenty of hell before that.

They scouted Bruckner's work detail for three days, studying the man's moves and

116

habits. The man seemed reasonably alert, that was one consideration. The other: the ground was wide open on both sides of the drainage ditch where the twenty or more prisoners had been laboring these past few days. Clearing a ditch that went where? Moon wasn't sure, unless it diverted water from the mine shafts. A slit trench came down out of a wash from the bald crest of a ridge. There were patches of owl clover on the slope, brittlebush and stubby clumps of mesquite and greasewood, but no cover to speak of.

Moon and his Mimbres talked it over in their dry camp and decided there was only one way to do the job.

Seven A.M., the seventeenth morning of Bren Early's incarceration, found him trudging up the grade with his shovel, second man in the file of prisoners – herded by four mounted guards, Bruckner bringing up the rear – Bren's eyes open as usual to scan the bleak terrain, now reaching the section of ditch they would be working today, moving up alongside it until Bruckner would stick two fingers in his mouth and whistle them to stop, jump in and commence digging and clearing.

Bren didn't see Moon. He didn't see the Mimbre Apaches – not until he heard that sharp whistle, the signal, turned to the trench and saw movement, a bush it looked like, a *bush* and part of the ground coming out out of the ditch, Christ, with a face made of dirt in it, seeing for the first time something he had only heard about: what it was like to stand in open terrain and, Christ, there they were all around you right *there* as you stood where there wasn't a sign of anything living a moment before. The Mimbres came out of the drainage ditch with greasewood in their hair, naked bodies smeared with dirt, and took the four deputies off their horses and had them on the ground, pointing revolvers in their struck-dumb faces before they knew what had happened. There were yells from the prisoners dancing around. Some of them raised their shovels and picks to beat the life out of Bruckner and his guards. But Moon had his stubby shotgun – Moon coming out of the ditch a few yards up the grade – would have none of it. He was not here in behalf of their freedom or revenge. They yelled some more and began to plead – Take us with you; don't leave us here – then cursed in loud voices, with the guards lying face down in the sand, calling Moon obscene names. But Moon never said a word to them or to anyone. Bren Early wanted to go over to Bruckner, but when Moon motioned, he followed. They rode out of

118

there on the deputies' horses and never looked back.

Bren Early went home with Moon, up past the white-washed agency buildings, up into the rugged east face of the Rincons. He saw Moon's stone house with its low adobe wall rimming the front of the property and its sweeping view of the San Pedro Valley. He saw Moon's wife in her light blue dress and white apron — no longer the McKean girl — saw the two cane chairs on the front porch and smelled the beef roast cooking.

"Well, now you have it, what do you do?" Bren said.

Moon looked at his wife and shrugged, not sure how to answer. "I don't know," he said, "get up in the morning and pull on my boots. How about you?"

"We'll see what happens, Bren said.

He rode out of there in borrowed clothes on a borrowed horse, but with visions of returning in relative splendor. Rich. At rest with himself. And with a glint in his eye that would say to Moon, "You *sure* you got what you want?"

Sweetmary: January, 1890

They were having their meeting in the stove-heated company office halfway up the grade, a wind blowing winter through the mine works: Bren Early, bearded, in his buffalo coat; Mr. Vandozen, looking like a banker in his velvet-lapeled Chesterfield and pinch-nose glasses; a man named Ross Selkirk, the superintendent of the Sweetmary works, who clenched a pipe in his jaw; and another company man, a geologist, by the name of Franklin Hovey.

Mr. Vandozen stood at a high table holding his glasses to his face as he looked over Bren Early's registered claims and assay reports. He said once, "There seems to be a question whether you're a miner, Mr. Early, or a speculator."

It wasn't a question he was waiting for, so Bren didn't answer.

Mr. Vandozen tried again. "Have you actually mined any ore?"

"Some."

"This one, I'll bet," Mr. Vandozen said, holding up an assay report. "Test would indicate quite a promising concentrate, as high as forty ounces to the ton."

"Three thousand dollars an ore-wagon load," Bren said.

And Mr. Vandozen said, "Before it's milled. On the deficit side you have labor, machinery, supplies, shipping, payments on your note —" The LaSalle Mining vice president, who had come all the way from New Mexico to meet Bren Early, looked over at him. "What do you have left?"

Not a question that required an answer. Bren waited.

"What you have, at best, are pockets of dust," Mr. Vandozen said. "Fast calculations in your head, multiplying ounces time thirty-five, I can understand how it lights up men's eyes. But obviously you don't want to scratch for a few ounces, Mr. Early, or you wouldn't be here."

Bren waited.

"Our geological surveys of your claims are" — Mr. Vandozen shrugged — "interesting, but by no means conclusive enough to warrant sinking shafts and moving in equipment. Though I'm sure you feel you have a major strike."

"Gold fever, it's called," the geologist said. "The symptoms are your eyes popping out of your head." He laughed, but no one else did.

Mr. Vandozen waited longer than he had to, following the interruption. When the office was quiet and they could hear the stove hissing and the wind gusting outside, he said, "We could give you — you have five claims? — all right, five thousand dollars for the lot and a one half of one percent royalty on gold ore after so many tons are milled."

"How much on all the copper ore I've got?"

The shaggy-looking prospector in the buffalo coat stopped everyone cold with the magic word.

It brought Mr. Vandozen's face up from the reports and claim documents to look at this Mr. Early again in a new light.

"You're telling us you have copper?"

"If your geologist knows it, you know it."

"It was my understanding you were only interested in gold."

"I'm interested in all manner of things," Bren said. "What are you interested in, besides high-grade copper?"

Mr. Vandozen took off his pinch-nose glasses and inspected them before putting them away, somewhere beneath his Chesterfield.

"How much do you want?"

There, that was the question. Bren smiled in his beard.

"Ten thousand dollars for the five claims," Mr. Vandozen said. "A two percent royalty on all minerals."

Bren shook his head.

At the fifty-thousand dollar offer he started for the door. At one-hundred thousand, plus royalties, plus a position with the company, the shaggy-looking miner-speculator stepped up to Mr. Vandozen and shook his hand. That part was done.

When the company superintendent, who was under Bren now in all matters except the actual operation of the mine, brought out a bottle of whiskey and said, "Mr. Early, I'll drink to your health but stay out of my way," Mr. Early looked at him and said:

"You run the works. There's only one area I plan to step into and I'm going to do it with both feet."

This shaggy-looking Bren Early entered the Gold Dollar with his buffalo coat draped over his left shoulder, covering his arm and hanging from shoulder to knee. He wore his Stetson, weathered now and shaped properly for all time, and his showy Merwin & Hulbert ivory-handled revolvers in worn-leather holsters. Business was humming for a cold and dismal afternoon, an hour before the day shift let out. The patrons, tending to their drinking and card playing, did not pay much attention to Bren at first. Not until he walked up behind the Sweetmary Deputy Sheriff who was hunched over the bar on his arms, and said to him:

"Mr. Bruckner?"

As the heavy-set man straightened and came around, Bren Early's right hand appeared from inside the buffalo coat with a pick handle, held short, and cracked it cleanly across the deputy sheriff's face.

Bruckner bellowed, fell sideways against the bar, came around with his great nose pouring blood and stopped dead, staring at Bren Early.

"Yes, you know me," Bren said, and swiped him again, hard, across the head.

Bruckner stumbled against the bar and this time came around with his right hand gripping his holstered Peacemaker. But caution stopped him in the nick of time from pulling it free. The left hand of this shaggy dude — standing like he was posing for a picture — was somewhere beneath that buffalo cape, and only the dude and God knew if he was holding a gun.

Bruckner said, "You're under arrest."

It was strange, Bren admired the remark. While the response from the Gold Dollar patrons was impromptu laughter, a short quick nervous fit of it, then silence. Bren was thinking, They don't know anything what it's like, do they?

He said to Bruckner then, "Wake up and listen to what I tell you. You're gonna pay me

124

eight dollars and fifty cents for the seventeen days I spent on your work gang. You're gonna pay everyone else now working whatever they've earned. You will never again use prisoners to do company work. And as soon as I'm through talking you're gonna go across the street and get my Smith forty-fours and bring them to me in their U.S. Army holsters. If I see you come back in here holding them by the grips or carrying any other weapon, I'll understand your intention and kill you before you get through the door. Now if you doubt or misunderstand anything I've said, go ask Ross Selkirk who the new boss is around here and he'll set you straight."

Bruckner took several moments to say, "I'll be back."

Let him have that much, a small shred of self-respect. The son of a bitch.

As the batwings swung closed, Bren stepped to the bar, lifting his buffalo coat and laying it across the polished surface. The patrons behind him stared and nudged each other. Look — both his revolvers were holstered.

Bren Early had come to Sweetmary.

125

Chapter VII

1

A news reporter told how he had knocked on the door one evening and when Mrs. Pierson opened it he said, "Excuse me, is this a whorehouse?" The woman said, "No, it isn't," not fazed a bit, and closed the door.

Someone else said, "It may not be a house for whores, but she is little better than one."

"Or better than most," another news reporter at the Gold Dollar said, "or he wouldn't have set her up as he did. She is a doggone good-looking woman."

None of the reporters had known about Mrs. Pierson until Maurice Dumas turned the first stone and then the rest of them began to dig. Maurice Dumas himself, once he saw where the story was leading,

126

backed off so as not to pry.

When the door of the house on Mill Street opened this time, the news reporter took off his hat and said, "Good afternoon, I'm William S. Wells, a journalist with the *St. Louis Globe-Democrat*. I'd like to ask you a few questions."

The good-looking dark-haired woman in the black dress stepped back to close the door. William S. Wells put his hand out, his foot already in place.

"Is it true Bren Early killed your son?"

Mrs. Pierson did not fight the door, though her hand remained on the knob. She looked at the journalist with little or no expression and said, "My son was killed while robbing the Benson stage by a passenger named Mr. DeLisle."

"If Bren Early did not kill your son," the journalist, Wells, said, "why did he buy this house for you?"

"He didn't buy this house for me."

"I understand he assumed the mortgage."

"Perhaps as an investment."

The journalist said, "Let's see now . . . the poor widow is running a boardinghouse, barely making ends meet following the death of her husband in a mill accident. Mr. Early comes along, pays off the note, gives you the deed to

127

the house and you get rid of the boarders so you can live here alone . . . some of the time alone, huh?" The journalist produced a little smile. "And you want me to believe he bought it as an *invest*ment?"

Mrs. Pierson said, "Do you think I care what you believe?"

"Bren Early was on the stage your boy tried to hold up. The same Bren Early who owns this house."

"I rent from him," Mrs. Pierson said.

"Yet you're a widow with no means of support."

"I have money my husband left."

"Uh-huh. Well, you must keep it under your mattress since you don't have a bank account either."

The journalist put on his grin as he stared at Mrs. Pierson — yes, a very handsome lady with her dark dark hair parted in the middle and drawn back in a bun — knowing he had her in a corner; then stopped grinning as the door opened wider and he was looking at Brendan Early, the man moving toward him into the doorway. The journalist said, "Oh —" not knowing Bren was here. He backed away, went down the three front steps to the walk and said then, "I see an old friend of yours is in town."

Bren said nothing as he slammed the door closed.

"Why were you telling him all that?"

"What did I tell him? He seemed to know everything."

"You sounded like you were going to stand there and answer anything he asked."

The woman shrugged. "What difference does it make?" and watched Bren as he moved from the door to a front window in the parlor. "You said yourself, let them think what they want."

Holding the lace curtains apart, looking out at the street of frame houses, he said, "We can't stop them from thinking, but we don't have to answer their questions."

"They don't have to ask much," she said. "It's your house — the arrangement is fairly obvious. But as long as it isn't spoken of out loud then it isn't improper. Is that it?"

Bren wore a white shirt, a dark tie and vest; his suitcoat hung draped over the back of a chair where his holstered revolvers rested on the seat cushion. He had been preparing to go out this afternoon after spending last night and this morning with her: preparing, grooming himself, looking at himself in the mirror solemnly as if performing a ritual.

As he turned from the window now to look at

129

her she waited, not knowing what he was going to say.

Then surprised her when he said, "Do I sound stuffy?"

She relaxed. "You sound grim, so serious."

"I'm not though. Not with you."

"No, the hard image you present to everyone else."

He came over to the chair where his coat was draped. "Maybe what I should do, put a notice in the paper. 'To Whom It May Concern . . . I'm the one wants to get married, she's the one wants to keep things as they are.' See what they ask you then."

"In other words," Janet Pierson said, "let them think what they want, as long as there's no doubt about your honor."

"I didn't mean it that way at all."

"But it's the way it is," the good-looking dark-haired woman said. "If you're going to spend your life standing on principle, you want to be sure everyone understands what the principle is."

He picked up his coat and pushed an arm into the sleeve. "You keep saying I worry about what people think of me, when I don't. All I said was, why tell that fella our personal business?"

"I'm sorry," she said. "You're right."

He pulled the coat down to fit smoothly as he turned to her. "I don't want you to say I'm *right*, I want to know what you're talking about."

"You get mad if I tell you what I feel."

He said, "Oh," and turned to the chair again to pick up his gunbelt and holsters.

"Are you coming back for supper?"

"I was planning on it. If we can have an evening without arguing."

"Are you pouting now?"

She shouldn't have said it — seeing his jaw tighten and hearing him say maybe he'd see her later, or maybe not — but sometimes she got tired of handling him so carefully, keeping him unruffled. Out in the street where he was going now, closing the door behind him, he was the legendary Bren Early who had shot and killed at least ten men who'd tested his nerve; a man whose posed photographs were displayed in the window of C.S. Fly's gallery on LaSalle Street and who was being written about by journalists from at least a dozen different newspapers. Bren Early: silent, deadly, absolutely true to his word.

But she could not help but think of a little boy playing guns.

He was a little boy sometimes when they were alone, unsure of himself.

131

He had come to her two and a half years ago, told her who he was and how he had met her son. He returned several times to visit, to sit in his parlor with her over coffee, and finally one day handed her the deed to the house – mortgage paid in full – asking nothing in return. Why?

He had not killed her son. A false rumor. He had, in fact, tried to prevent her son's death. But had failed and perhaps it was that simple: he felt responsible, owed her something because of his failure. He had said, "Don't ask questions. I like you, I want to do something for you." All right, and she liked him and it was easy enough to take the sign down and change the boardinghouse back to a residence. It seemed to happen naturally as they saw more of each other. He wanted a woman in town and she responded. Why not? She liked him enough.

Janet Pierson, at forty, was at least five years older then Bren. She was attractive, had maintained her slim figure, they enjoyed one another; so age was not a consideration. Until he said he wanted to marry her.

She asked why and felt early suspicions aroused. He said he wanted to marry her, that was why in itself; he loved her. Yes, he had said he loved her. And he had also said, many times,

"You think too much," when she told him he really didn't want to marry her but felt an obligation or was afraid of what people thought. He had said over and over that people had nothing to do with it, goddamn it, *people* could think whatever they wanted; what *he* wanted was to be married to her. Then she had said the words that made him stare at her and then frown, perplexed, and finally get angry, the words he would never understand and she couldn't seem to explain.

She had said, "I think what you want to do is take the place of my son. You want to make up his loss."

And he had said, "You believe I think of you as my *mother?*"

Yes, but she would not admit that to him: the little boy who came in the house when he was finished playing his role on the street. She didn't understand it herself, she only felt it. So she referred to him being like a little boy without referring to herself as a mother or using the word.

There was risk involved, to tell the man who had been a cavalry officer and had stood his ground and shot ten men, that he was still, deep down, a little boy and wanted his own way. He would pound his fist down or storm out (See? she would say to herself), then calm down or come back in a little while and say, "How do you get ideas like that?"

And she would say, "I just know."

"Because you had a son? Listen, maybe what you're doing, you're still playing mama, Jesus Christ, and you're using *me*. I'm not doing it, *you* are."

Blaming her. Then saying he loved her and wanted to marry her and be with her always. Yet they very seldom went out of the house as a couple. Sitting together in a restaurant he was obviously self-conscious; as though being seen with her revealed a vulnerable, softer side of him. The only thing she was certain of: Bren Early didn't know what he wanted.

2

Maurice Dumas stood in the doorway of the Chinaman's place on Second Street. He had been waiting an hour and a half, watching toward Mill Street and, every once in a while, looking in at the empty restaurant wondering how the Chinaman stayed in business . . . then wondering if Mr. Early had forgot or had changed his mind. Twice he'd run back to the corner of Second and LaSalle and looked across

134

the street toward the Congress Hotel. The news reporters were still waiting on the porch.

When finally he saw Early coming this way from Mill Street, Maurice Dumas felt almost overwhelming relief. In the time it took Early to reach him — Early looking neat and fresh though it was quite warm this afternoon in May — Maurice Dumas had time to compose himself.

He nodded and said, "Mr. Early."

"He arrive?"

"Yes sir, on the noon shuttle from Benson."

"Alone?"

"I believe there was a Mexican gentleman with him."

It was something to stand close to this man and watch him in unguarded moments, watch him think and make decisions that would become news stories — like watching history being made.

"They went up to the mine office first and then to the hotel," Maurice said, "I guess where he's staying. Everybody thinks you're there, too, I guess. Or will come there. So they expect the hotel is where it'll happen — if it's gonna."

Bren Early thought a little more before saying, "Go see him. Tell him you spoke to me." He paused. "Tell him I'll be in this quiet place out of the sun if he wants to have a word with me."

It was the Mexican, Ruben Vega, who came to the Chinaman's place. He greeted Early, nodding and smiling as he joined him at a back table, away from the sun glare on the windows. They could have been two old friends meeting here in the empty restaurant, though Bren Early said nothing at first because he was surprised. He felt it strange that he was glad to see this man who was smiling warmly and telling him he had not changed one bit since that time at the wall in Sonora. It was strange, too, Bren felt, that he recognized the man immediately and could tell that the man had changed; he was older and looked older, with a beard now that was streaked with gray.

"Man," Ruben Vega said, "the most intelligent thing I ever did in my life, I didn't walk up to the wall with them. . . . You not drinking nothing?"

"Is he coming?" asked Bren.

"No, he's not coming. He sent me to tell you he isn't angry, it was too long ago." The Mexican looked around, saying then, "Don't they have nothing to drink in this place?"

They sent Maurice Dumas out to get a bottle of *mescal*, which the Mexican said he was thirsty for. Bren had beer, served by the China-man, and drank several glasses of it while they talked, allowing Maurice to sit with them but not paying any attention to him, until he tried the *mescal* and made a terrible face and the Mexican said to Bren, "Your friend don't know what's good."

"If you like a drink that tastes like poison candy," Bren said, though he tried a short glass of it to see if it was still as bad as he remembered it was the first time he drank it in the sutler's store at Huachuca. "That could kill you," he said.

"No, but walking up to the wall where you and other one stood, that would have," Ruben Vega said.

"You might have made the difference," Bren said.

"Maybe I would have shot one of you, I don't know. But something told me it would be my last day on earth."

"How did you keep him alive?"

The Mexican shrugged. "Tied him to a horse. He kept himself alive to Morelos. Then in the infirmary they cleaned him, sewed him together. He has a hole here," Ruben Vega said, touching his cheek, "some teeth missing" – he grinned – "part of his ear. But he's no more ugly than he was before. See, the ugliness is inside him. I say to him, 'Man, what is it like to be you? To live inside your body?' He don't know what I'm talking about. I say to him, 'Why don't you be tranquil and enjoy life more instead of rubbing against it?' He still don't know what I'm talking about, so I leave him alone . . . Well, let me think. Why didn't he die? I don't know. From Morelos I took him to my old home at Bavispe, then down to Hermosillo . . . Guaymas, we looked at the sea and ate fish . . . a long way around to come back here, but only in the beginning he was anxious to go back and saying what he's going to do to you when he finds you."

"Others tried," Bren said.

"Yes, we hear that. Then time pass, he stop talking about it. We do some work in New Mexico for a mine company, bring them beef. Then do other work for them, make more money than before." The Mexican shrugged again. "He's not so ugly inside now."

"He must've paid you pretty well," Bren said. "You stay with him."

"I'll tell you the truth, I almost left him by the wall in Sonora, but I work for his family, his father before him. Yes, Sundeen always pay me pretty well as segundo. If I'm going to be in that business, stealing cows, running them across the border, I'm not very particular who I

138

work with, uh? But he isn't so bad now. He doesn't talk so much as he used to."

Bren said, "How's he look at this job he's got?"

"Well, we just come here. He has some men coming the company hired. I guess we go up and drive those people off. What else?" He raised his *mescal* glass, then paused. "But we hear your friend is up there too, the other one from the wall. How is it you're here and he's up there, your friend?"

"It's the way it is, that's all," Bren said. "This land situation, who owns what, is none of my business."

"You don't care then," Ruben Vega said, "we go up there and run him off."

Maurice Dumas' gaze moved from the Mexican to Bren Early and waited for the answer.

"You say run him off and make it sound easy," Bren said. "It isn't a question of whether I care or not, have an interest, it's whether you can do it and come back in one piece. I'm like Maurice here and all the rest. Just a spectator."

3

It was after five o'clock when Ruben Vega

139

returned to the Congress Hotel. The men who had been pointed out to him as journalists and not a part of a business convention were still on the front porch and in the lobby. They stopped talking when he came in, but no one called to him or said anything.

He mentioned it to Sundeen who stood at the full-length mirror in his room, bare to the waist, turning his head slowly, studying himself as he trimmed his beard.

"They know I come with you, but they don't ask me anything. You know why?"

"Why?" Sundeen said to himself in the mirror.

"Because they think I shine your shoes, run errands for you."

"You saw him?"

"Yes, I talk to him, tell him you're not mad no more."

"Wavy-haired son of a bitch. He look down his nose at you?"

"A little, holding back, not saying much. But he's all right. Maybe the same as you are."

Sundeen trimmed carefully with the scissors, using a comb to cover the deep scar in his left cheek where hair did not grow and was like an indentation made with a finger that remained when the finger was withdrawn, the skin around the hole tight and shiny.

"Instead of what you think," Sundeen said, "tell me what he had to say."

"He say it's none of his business. He's going to watch."

"You believe it?"

"Now you want to know what I think. Make up your mind."

Sundeen half turned to the mirror to study his profile, smoothing his beard with the back of his hand. "His partner's up there, but he's gonna keep his nose out of it, huh?"

Yes, they may be somewhat alike, Ruben Vega thought. He said, "The company pay him to work here, whatever he does, not to go up there and help his friend. So maybe he doesn't have the choice to make."

"What does he say about Moon?"

"Nothing. I ask, do you see him? No. I say, why don't they leave instead of causing this trouble? He say, ask them. I say well, he likes to live on a mountain — there plenty other mountains. He don't say anything. I say, what about the other people up there, they live with him? He say, you find out."

Sundeen looked at his body, sucking in his stomach, then picked up a shirt from the chair and put it on. "I think somebody's selling somebody a bill of goods. All we have to say to them is, look here, you people don't move out,

141

this is what happens to you. Take one of 'em, stick a gun in his mouth and count three. They'll leave."

"Take which one?"

"It don't matter to me none. 'Cept it won't be Moon. Moon, I'm gonna settle with him. Early too. But I got time to think about that."

Ruben Vega was nodding. "Threaten them seriously — it look pretty easy, uh?"

"Not hard or easy but a fact of life," Sundeen said. "Nobody picks dying when there's a way not to."

Ruben Vega would agree to that. He could say to his boss, And it works both ways, for you as well as them. But why argue about it with a man who did not know how to get outside of himself to look at something? It had happened to him at the wall. It could happen to him again. Ruben Vega said, "Well, I hope you get enough men to do it."

Sundeen said, "Wait and see what's coming."

It was already arranged, since his meeting with Vandozen in Las Cruces, Vandozen asking how many men he'd need. Sundeen saying he'd wait and see. Vandozen then saying it was his custom to know things in advance, not wait and see. So he had already recruited some twenty men, among them several former Yuma prison guards, a few railroad bulls and good number of strikebreakers from the coal fields of Pennsylvania: all hired at twenty dollars a week and looking forward to a tour of duty out in the fresh air and wide open spaces.

Today was Tuesday. A message waiting for Sundeen when he reported to the company stated his bunch would all arrive in Benson by rail on Friday. Fine. Let them get drunk and laid on Saturday, rest Sunday and they ride up into the mountains on Monday.

Sundeen said to the Mexican, "If that's all you got, you didn't learn much."

"He thought you were dead," Ruben Vega said. "I told him you should be, but you stayed alive and now you're much wiser."

Looking at him Sundeen said, "The fencesitter. You gonna sit on the fence and watch this one too? Man, that time in Sonora — I swore I was gonna kill you after, if I hadn't been shot up."

"I save your life you feel you want to kill me," Ruben Vega said. "I think you still have something to learn."

4

Bren had not realized he was tense. Until walking back to the house on Mill Street he was aware of relief and was anxious to be with the woman again. He had not told her about Sundeen. He didn't like to argue with her or discuss serious matters. She was a woman and he wanted her to act like a woman, one he had selected. He did not expect continual expressions of gratitude; nor did he want her to wait on him or act as though her life was now dedicated solely to his pleasure. But she could make his life easier if she'd quit assuming she knew more about him than he did. Women were said to "know" and feel things men weren't able to because men were more blunt and practical. Bren believed that was a lot of horse shit. Women took advantage of men because they were all sitting on something men wanted. If they ever quit holding out or holding it over men's heads everybody would be a lot happier.

Not that Janet Pierson ever bargained with him that way. She seemed always willing and eager. He only wished she would quit thinking and analyzing why he did things and saying he wanted to be like a son to her.

Sometimes though he would bring it up, because it was on his mind or to convince her she was wrong — as he did now, entering the front door and hearing her in the kitchen, coming up quietly behind her, pulling her into his arms, his hands moving over her body.

"I missed you," she said, resting against him.

"I missed you too. You think I'd do this to my mother?"

"I hope not."

"Unh-unh." Kissing her now, brushing her cheek and finding her ear with his mouth. "No . . . What you feel like to me is a young girl . . . soft and nice —"

She said, pressing against him, "That's what I feel. You make me aware of being a woman and it's a good feeling." This way acknowledging and appreciating him as a man, but knowing that what he needed now was to be comforted and held. Protected from something. The little boy come home — but not telling him this.

After they made love she would put her arms around him and hold him close to her in the silence and soon he would fall asleep. Then, as she would begin to ease her arm from beneath his shoulder, he would open his eyes for a moment, roll to his side and fall asleep again, freeing her. Though if she moved her hand over him, down over the taut muscles in his belly, they would make love again and after, this time, he would get out of bed as Bren Early: confident, the man who wore matched revolvers and loved her when it occurred to him

to express it or when he felt the physical urge
. . . not realizing the simple need to hold and
be held and to believe in something other than
himself.

Sometime soon she would talk to him and
find out what he believed and what was important to him. And what was important to her
also.

5

Was it luck or was it instinct? Maurice Dumas hoped the latter. There was always something going on when he set out to get a story:
this time not at the White Tanks agency but
several miles up the draw at Dana Moon's
place.

The luck was running into the Apache at the
agency office and letting him know through
sign language — trying all kinds of motions
before pointing to the office and then sticking
his tongue in his cheek to resemble a wad of
tobacco — that he was looking for the agent,
Dana Moon.

They climbed switchbacks up a slope swept
yellow-green with brittlebush and greasewood,
through young saguaros that looked like a field

146

of fence posts and on up into the wide, yawning trough of a barranca with steep walls of shale and wind-swept white oak and cedar. They climbed to open terrain, a bare crest against the sky but not the top, not yet. A little farther and there it was, finally, a wall . . . first the wall, and beyond it a low stone fortress of a house with a wooden porch and a yard full of people, horses and several wagons.

What was this, another Meat Day?

No, Maurice Dumas found out soon enough, it was a war council.

He felt strange riding in through the opening in the adobe wall with all eyes on him. Though there were not as many people as he originally thought — only about a dozen — they were certainly a colorful and unusual mixture: darkies, Mexicans and Indians, all standing around together and all, he observed now, armed to the teeth with revolvers, rifles and belts of cartridges. Specifically there were three hard-looking colored men; four Mexicans, one in a very large Chichuhua hat and bright yellow scarf; and the rest Apache Indians, including the one who brought him up here and who, Maurice Dumas found out, was named Red, an old compadre of Moon's.

"I hope I'm not interrupting anything," Maurice Dumas said, as Moon came down

147

from the porch to greet him, "but there is something I think you better know about."

"Sundeen's arrival?" said Moon, who almost smiled then at the young reporter's look of surprise. "There are things we better know about if we intend to stay here. Have his men arrived yet?"

Maurice Dumas, again surprised, said, "What men?"

"You'd know if they had," Moon said. "So, we still have some time. Step down and I'll introduce you to some of the main characters of the story you're gonna be writing."

The man seemed so aware and alert for someone who moved the way Moon did, hands in his pockets, in no hurry, big chew of tobacco in his jaw: just a plain country fellow among this colorful group of heavily armed neighbors.

First, Maurice Dumas met Mrs. Moon, Kate, and felt he must have appeared stupid when he looked up and saw a good-looking lady and not the washed-out, sodbuster woman he'd expected. When she learned where he was from, Mrs. Moon said, "Chicago, huh? I'll bet you're glad to get away from the stockyards and breathe fresh air for a change."

The news reporter said he didn't live near the yards, fortunately, and noticed Moon looking at his wife with an amused expression and then shaking his head; just a faint movement. The man seemed to get a kick out of her. He said, "What do you know about Chicago stockyards?" She answered him, "I visited there with my dad when I was little and have never felt the urge to go back." Strange, having a conversation like that in front of everyone.

Moon said, "Maurice, shake hands with a veteran of the War of the Rebellion and a cavalryman twenty-four years."

This was the young reporter's introduction to Bo Catlett, whom he had already heard about and who did not disappoint him in his appearance, with his high boots and felt campaign hat low over his eyes. Bo Catlett's expression was kindly, yet he was mean and hard-looking in that he seemed the type who would never hold his hat in his hand and stand aside or give an inch, certainly not give up his horse ranch. The other two colored men wore boots also, standing the way cavalrymen seem to pose, and appeared just as fit and ready as Bo Catlett. There were three more former members of the Tenth up with their families or tending the herds.

Red, the little Mimbre Apache, said something in Spanish to Moon and Moon said, "He thought, when you rode up and commenced making signs, you were asking him how old he

149

was, how many moons, till you stuck your tongue in your cheek."

The Apaches sat along the edge of the porch, Maurice Dumas noticed, while all the others stood around. (Did it mean Indians were lazy by nature?, Maurice wondered. Or smart enough to squat when they got the chance?)

The news reporter wouldn't have minded sitting down himself in one of those cane rocking chairs. But first he had to meet Armando Duro — and his young son Eladio who was about eighteen — and this introduction turned into something he never expected.

Maurice had a feeling Moon had saved Armando until last out of deference, for he seemed especially polite and careful as he addressed him in Spanish, nodding toward Maurice as Maurice caught the words *Chicago Times*. Was the Mexican impressed?

The young news reporter was, for he had heard the name Armando Duro before, though he had not known this fiery champion of Mexican land rights was living in these mountains.

Here he was now rattling off Spanish a mile a minute, his son and his companions nodding in agreement while Moon listened intently at first, then seemed to get tired of hanging on and shifted his weight from one foot to the other as Armando went on and on. When there was a pause Maurice said quickly, "I'd like to interview Señor Duro if I could."

Moon said, "If you can get a word in." Armando's eyes darted from the news reporter to Moon. "And if you — *si puede hablar en Español*. Can you?"

"Doesn't he speak English?"

"When he wants to," Moon said. "It depends if he's in one of his royal pain-in-the-ass moods or not."

If the Mexican could understand him, how come Moon was saying this in front of him? Evidently because Moon had only so much patience with the man and had run out.

Following Moon's less than kind remark, Armando turned to the young news reporter and said in English, "Will you print the truth for a change if I give it to you?"

What kind of question was that? Maurice Dumas said the *Times* always printed the truth.

"The twisting of truth to fit your purpose," Armando said, "is the same as a lie."

Maurice didn't know what the man was talking about because the paper had hardly ever printed anything about Armando Duro or Mexican land rights to begin with. It was an old issue, settled in court, dead and buried. But since the man did represent the Mexican com-

151

munity here, some eighty or ninety people living on scattered farms and sheep pastures, Maurice decided he'd better pay attention.

He said, "Well, I suppose you see this present situation as an opportunity to air your complaints once again, bring them into the open." Maurice heard Moon groan and knew he had said the wrong thing.

Sure enough.

Armando started talking, taking them back to the time of Spanish land grants and plodding on through the war with Mexico and the Gadsen Purchase to explain why their acreage, their sheep graze, their golden fields of corn and bean patches belonged to them as if by divine succession and not to a mining company from a state named for a small island in the English Channel (which Maurice Dumas had not realized before this).

Bo Catlett and the colored troopers shuffled around or leaned against a wagon. Moon would continue to shift from one foot to another. His wife, what she did was shake her head and go into the house. Even Armando's son and the other Mexicans seemed ready to fall asleep. Only the Apaches, sitting along the edge of the porch, stared at Armando with rapt attention, not having any idea what he was talking about, even though Armando would lapse into fiery

Spanish phrases every so often. He reminded the young news reporter of every politician he had ever heard speak, except that Armando talked in bigger circles that included God and kings.

"How am I going to write about all that?" Maurice said to Moon, after.

Moon said, "You picked your line of work, I didn't."

Armando got a rolled-up sheet of heavy paper from his wagon and came over to the news reporter opening it as you would a proclamation, which is what it was.

"Here," Armando said, handing it to Maurice, "show this to the mine company and print it in your newspaper so anyone who sees one of these will know it marks the boundary of our land."

The notice said, in large black letters:

WARNING

Anyone venturing into
this land uninvited is

TRESPASSING

on property granted by
Royal Decree and witnessed

before God. Trespassers
are not welcome and will
be fired on if they cross this boundary.
Armando Duro
and the
People of the Mountain

Later on, just before Maurice Dumas left to
go back down the switchback trail, he said
to Moon, "Does that man know what he's
doing?"

"It's his idea of the way to do it," Moon said.

"But that warning's not gonna do any good.
You think?"

"Warning?" Moon said. "It reads more like an
invitation."

"Can't you stop him, shut him up?"

"I suppose," Moon said, "but the sooner it
starts, the sooner it's over, huh?"

6

Moon, Bo Catlett and Red, the leader of the
Mimbres, packed up into the high reaches to
shoot some game, drink whiskey, have a talk
and get away from their women for a few days.
Moon said that's all they would have, three

154

days. On the piney shoulder of the mountain where they camped, they could hear the mine company survey crew exploding dynamite as they searched out new ore veins: like artillery off to the west, an army gradually moving closer, having already wiped out several of the Mexican homesites.

Armando Duro had drawn the line and posted his trespass notices, giving himself a printed excuse to start shooting. But how did you tell a man like Armando he was a fool? Armando was not a listener, he was a talker.

Moon, in the high camp, took out a rough-sketch map he'd drawn and laid it on the pine needles for Bo Catlett and Red to look at, Moon pointing: little squares were homes and farms, though maybe he was missing some; the circles were graze. X's marked the areas where the survey crews had been working.

Here, scattered over the pastureland in the Western foothills, the Mexican homesteads. How would you defend them?

"No way to do it, considering they farmers," Bo Catlett said. "They ever see more than three coming they got to get out . . . Maybe try draw them up in the woods."

Moon shook his head. "Armando told them, don't leave your homes. Something about leaving your honor on the doorstep when you flee."

"I'm not talking about they should *flee*," Bo Catlett said. "But they start shooting from the house, that's where they gonna die. They don't have enough people in one place. Like you —" Bo Catlett looked at the map. "Where you at here?"

Moon pointed to the square on the Eastern slope, the closest one to the wavy line indicating the San Pedro River.

"You no better off'n they are," Bo Catlett said, "all by yourself there."

"I got open ground in front of me and high rock behind," Moon said, "with Red and some of his people right here, watching my back door. Nobody gets close without my knowing. So . . . around here, both sides of the crest, the Apache rancherías. Red, that's you right there. Coming south a bit, these circles are the horse pastures . . . Here's the canyon, Bo, where you got your settlement."

"Niggerville," Bo Catlett said. "Some day they put railroad tracks up there, you can bet money we be on the wrong side."

"Here's the box canyon," Moon continued, "where you gather your mustangs. I'm thinking we might do something with that blind alley. You follow me?"

"Invite 'em in," Bo Catlett said, "and close the door."

"It'd be a way, wouldn't it? If they come up to Niggerville and you pull back, draw 'em into the box."

"If they dumb enough, think I'm a black lead mare," Bo Catlett said.

"We'll find out," Moon said. "Red's gonna be our eyes, huh, Red? *Los ojos.*" And said in Spanish, "The eyes of the mountain people."

The Apache nodded and said, also in Spanish, "It's been a long time since we used them."

Moon said, "Him and a bunch were gonna summer up at Whiteriver, visit some of their people, but Red's staying now for the war. That's what they call it in town, the Rincon Mountain War."

Bo Catlett seemed to be thinking about the name, trying it a few times in his mind. "We got any say in it?"

"We're still around when the smoke clears," Moon said, "I guess we can still call it anything we want."

Chapter VIII

1

Phil Sundeen looked at the notice with the big word "WARNING" at the top like it was a birthday present he had always wanted. He read it slowly, came down to Armando's name at the bottom, said, "That's the one I want," and sent Ruben Vega out on a scout, see if the notices were "for true."

That Monday morning Ruben Vega rode a fifteen-mile loop through the west foothills, spotting the little adobes tucked away up on the slopes; seeing the planted fields, young corn not quite belly-high to his horse; seeing the notices stuck to saguaro and white oak and three times drawing rifle fire — Ruben Vega squinting up at the high rocks as the reports faded, then shaking

158

his head and continuing on.

He made his way up through a mesquite thicket that followed the course of a draw to a point where he could study one of the videttes crouched high in the rocks, skylined for all to see, a young man in white with an old single-shot Springfield, defending his land. Ruben Vega, dismounted, circled behind the vidette to within forty feet and called out, *"Dígame!"*

The young man in white came around, saw the bearded man holding a revolver and fired his Springfield too quickly, without taking time to aim.

Ruben Vega raised his revolver. "Tell me where I can find Armando Duro."

Thirty dollars a week to frighten this young farmer and others like him. It was a pity. Ruben Vega said to the man, who was terrified but trying to act brave, he only wanted to speak to Armando Duro and needed directions to his house. That was all. He nodded, listening to the young farmer, holstered his gun and left.

Yes, he told Sundeen, the notices were "for real."

"They shoot at you?"

"They don't know what they're doing."

"I *know* that," Sundeen said. "I want to know if they're good for their word." When Ruben Vega told him yes, they had fired, though not to hit him, Sundeen said, "All right, let's go."

He paraded out his security force: his prison guards, railroad bulls and strikebreakers; most of whom wore city clothes and looked like workingmen on Sunday, not one under thirty years of age, Ruben Vega noticed. Very hard men with big fists, bellies full of beer and whiskey from their first weekend in town, armed with Winchester repeaters and revolvers stuck in their belts. Sixteen of them: two had quit by Monday saying it was too hot and dusty, the hell with it. One was dead of knife wounds and the one who had killed him was in jail. Ruben Vega knew he would never be their segundo, because these men would never do what a Mexican told them. But that was all right. They could take orders directly from Sundeen. Ruben Vega would scout for them, stay out of their way and draw his thirty dollars a week — the most he had ever made in his life — which would make these men even uglier if they knew the Mexican was being paid more than they were. But he didn't like this work. From the beginning he had not liked it at all.

He didn't like Sundeen waving off the few news reporters — one of them the young one who had been with Early — who had hired horses and wanted to follow. He didn't like it because it surprised him — Sundeen not wanting them along to write about them.

He asked, "Why not bring them?"

"Not this trip," Sundeen said. "Get up there and show us the way, partner."

Ruben Vega followed his orders and rode point, guiding Sundeen and his security force up into the hills where the WARNING notices were nailed to the saguaro and white oak. There. Now Sundeen could do what he wanted.

Looking over his crew of bulls and headbusters sweating in their Sunday suits, the crew squinting up at the high rock formations, Sundeen said, "Who wants to do the honors, chase their pickets off that high ground? I'd say there's no more'n likely two of 'em up there — couple of bean farmers couldn't hit shit if they stuck their weapons up their ass. How about you, you and you?" And said to the others, "Get ready now."

More than two, Ruben Vega thought, because they know we're coming to see Armando. Maybe all the guns they have are up there now. Guarding the pass to the man's house. Ruben Vega nudged his mount up next to Sundeen's.

"They'll have plenty guns up there," he said quietly.

Sundeen turned in his saddle to look at him and smiled as he spoke, as though he was

161

talking about something else. "We don't know till we see, partner. Till we draw fire, huh?" Then to the three he had picked: "Go on up past the signs."

Another show to watch, Ruben Vega thought, seeing the three men moving their horses at a walk up through the ocotillo and yellow-flowering prickly pear, reaching the sign nailed to a saguaro . . . moving past the cactus . . . twenty feet perhaps, thirty, when the gunfire poured out of the rocks a hundred yards away: ten, a dozen rifles, Ruben Vega estimated, fired on the count, but the eruption of sound coming raggedly with puffs of smoke and followed by three single shots that chased the two riders still mounted, both of them bent low in their saddles and circling back. One man in his Sunday suit lay on the ground, out there alone now, his riderless horse running free. The one on the ground didn't move. Sundeen was yelling at his security force to commence firing. Then yelled at them to spread out as their horses began to shy and bump each other with the rifles going off close. "Spread out and rush 'em!" Sundeen yelled, pointing and then circling around to make sure they were all moving forward . . . Ruben Vega watching, wondering if Sundeen knew what he was doing . . . Sundeen pausing then as his

162

men charged up the slope firing away . . . Ruben Vega impressed now that these dressed-up shitkickers would do what they were told and expose themselves to fire. Sundeen hung back, grinning as he looked over at Ruben Vega now sitting motionless in his saddle.

"Still riding the fence, huh?"

Ruben Vega said, "Well, you got a man killed."

"Three'd be better," Sundeen said, "but one's enough to inspire them."

It didn't take much to push the farmers out of the rocks. They reloaded and got off a volley, hitting nothing, then fell back from the steady fire of the Winchester repeaters, some of them running, others making their way back to Armando Duro's place where they would be forced to make a stand.

Sundeen and his people circled to high ground and found good cover in a fairly deep wash rimmed with brush. From here they looked down on Armando's house and yard: a whitewashed adobe with a roof of red clay tiles that had come from an old church in Tucson, a flower garden, a latticework covered with green vines, heavy shutters with round gunports over the windows. A snug cottage with thick walls up here in the lonesome.

Sundeen said, "Well, we can starve him out

or maybe set the place on fire, but we'd never get home for supper, would we?" From a saddle bag he pulled out a towel with *Congress Hotel* printed on it and threw it to Ruben Vega, saying, "Hey, partner, make yourself useful."

Tied to a mesquite pole the towel was the truce flag Ruben Vega waved above the brush cover and held high in front of him as he walked down to the yard, unarmed, doing something for his thirty dollars a week.

He called to the house in Spanish, "Do I address Armando Duro? . . . Look, I have no gun. Will you come out, please, and talk like a gentleman? We have no fight with you. We come to talk and you begin shooting." He paused. "Before anyone else is injured please come talk to the man sent by the company. He has something important to explain."

"Say it now," a voice from the house said.

"I'm not the emissary of the company," Ruben Vega said. "Mr. Sundeen is the one. He wants to explain the company plan of making this a township . . . if you would honor us and agree to become the alcalde and administer the office."

"Where is he?" the voice asked.

"You come out and he'll come out," Ruben Vega said, beginning to feel relief now, knowing he was almost finished.

There was a long pause, silence, before the voice said again, "Where is he?"

"Up there," Ruben Vega said, pointing with his truce flag.

"He must come with no weapons. All of them must show themselves with no weapons," the voice said.

"Of course," Ruben Vega said, thinking, He's a child; you could offer him candy. As he saw the door open, Ruben Vega began to move away, turning to wave to Sundeen to come down, calling out, "All right . . . Come with your hands in the air, please!" Looking back at the house, still moving off to the side, he said in Spanish, "Your men come out too, please, everyone without weapons. We meet at this sign of truce and speak as gentlemen," thinking, Yes, isn't it a nice day and everybody's friends . . . Smile . . . but get your old ass out of the way as soon as you can, without hurrying, but move it.

2

Moon handed the glasses to Bo Catlett and picked up his Sharps rifle from the Y of the cliffrose branch in front of him.

"They all got *suits* on," Bo Catlett said, with the field glasses to his face "Coming with their hands in the air. They sur*ren*dering?"

"You see the white flag?" Moon said.

"Man moving out of the way."

"I saw him do it once before," Moon said, "Something like this. What would you say's the range?"

From this position, where Moon and Bo Catlett, Red and three of his Mimbres crouched in the outcropping of rock and flowering cliffrose — high up on a slope of scrub pine — they had a long downview of the red-tile postage-stamp roof of the house and the tiny dark figures coming down to the yard, approaching the tiny figures in white coming out of the house.

Bo Catlett continued to study the scene through the field glasses, saying now, "You got . . . three hundred fifty yards 'tween us and them."

"Close," Moon said, "but more like four hundred," and sighted down the barrel of the Sharps. "It looks shorter aiming down." He lowered the big-bore rifle to adjust the rear sight and put it to his shoulder again to aim, both eyes open.

"Wearing suits," Bo Catlett was saying. "All dressed up to pay a visit, huh?"

166

Moon said something in slow Spanish, as though explaining carefully, and the Mimbres raised their Springfields and Spencers. He waited a moment and then said, *"Listo?"*

The Mimbres were ready. Bo Catlett continued to watch through the glasses.

"The one with the silver belt buckles," Moon said.

"His holsters empty," Bo Catlett said. "None of them appear armed."

"Come up here with their coats on," Moon said, "account of it's so cold. Only about ninety degrees out. Watch Sundeen, he'll do something. Take off his hat, something to give 'em a sign."

"Talking," Bo Catlett said. "Moving around some . . . Mexicans standing there listening to him, Armando, shit, look at him with his big hat on, arms folded, standing there . . . Sundeen looking up at the sky now, looking around . . . looking back at Armando . . . hey, yelling something . . . they drawing *guns!* He going for the Mexican!"

Moon fired.

The Mimbres fired.

The sounds of hitting hard and flat in the stillness, echoing . . . the hard sounds hitting again, almost covering the popping sounds of pistol fire coming from the yard, where tiny dark figures and tiny white figures were left lying on the ground as the lines of figures began to come apart and scatter. The rifles echoed again, cracking the hot air hard, and in a moment the yard was empty but for the figures lying motionless: three dark figures, four white figures. A single white figure was being dragged, carried off by a crowd of dark figures.

Bo Catlett followed them through the glasses until they were out of sight, beyond a rise and a line of brush. He wasn't sure which one they'd dragged off until his gaze inched back to the yard, past the figures lying there, and saw the big Mexican hat on the ground.

"They got Armando," Bo Catlett said.

3

C.S. "Buck" Fly, who was a gentleman and had never been known to say an unkind word about anyone, paused and said, "I already shot that rooster."

"We went to very much trouble to get him," Ruben Vega said. "Rode all the way up there to talk to him."

"Is he coming here?" C.S. Fly asked, not

168

wanting to give the Mexican a flat no, but not wanting to take the other Mexican's picture either. The other Mexican, Armando, was impatient and difficult to pose, because he thought he knew everything, including photography. C.S. Fly also had a lot on his mind. His wife was in Tombstone, where business was not too good; he had opened a gallery in Phoenix that wasn't doing much better; there was not much going on here in Sweetmary at the moment; and he was trying to make up his mind whether or not he should run for sheriff of Cochise County on the Republican ticket next year, as some of his friends were urging him to do. What did he want to take a picture of a pompous, officious Mexican land-granter for?

"You have to bring your picture machine to where he is. I'll show you," Ruben Vega said.

"Well, as I've mentioned, I already have Armando on file," Mr. Fly said. "One of him is plenty."

"But do you have him talking to Mr. Sundeen of the mine company, settling the difference between them, the two sides shaking hands in a picture you can sell to all the newspapers in the country?" Ruben Vega asked.

"No, I don't believe I have that one," C.S. Fly said. "Where is it they're meeting?"

169

Ruben Vega told him, a ranch out of town only a few miles, the J-L-Bar, owned by a man named Freels, a neutral ground between the mine and the mountains. Mr. Fly said all right, had his assistant load camera and equipment on a buckboard and they were on their way — heading out LaSalle Street, when the young news reporter Ruben Vega had met before rode up to join them, asking what was going on. Ruben Vega had said come on, and asked where the other reporters were. (Sundeen had not said anything this time about keeping reporters away.) The young fellow from Chicago, Maurice Dumas, said they most always took a nap after their noon dinner and that's probably where they were. When he asked where they were going, Ruben Vega told him Mr. Fly was going to take a picture of an important occasion, a meeting between Sundeen and Armando.

Because his luck or intuition had been so keen lately, Maurice Dumas believed him, patting his pocket to make sure he had a pad and pencil. It looked like another *Chicago Times* exclusive coming up.

About three miles out of town, having come around a bend in the road that was banked close to a steep slope — with still a mile or so to go before reaching the J-L-Bar ranch — they saw something white hanging from a telegraph pole.

Was it a flag of some kind? There was no wind stirring it. As they approached, seeing it straight down the road now, maybe a hundred yards away, Maurice Dumas thought of a bag of laundry. Or, could it be a mail bag out by the Freels place? Something white — as they drew closer — tied to the pole about ten feet off the ground . . . No, not tied to the pole, hanging from a rope . . . Not a bag of laundry either. A man. Maurice Dumas heard the Mexican say something in Spanish. He heard C.S. Fly say, "Oh, my God."

It was Armando Duro, hung there by the neck, the rope reaching up and over the cross-bar where the wires were attached and down to the base of the pole where the rope was lashed securely. Armando's head hung down, chin on his chest, his face so dark he looked like a Negro — which was why Maurice was not sure at first who it was. His hands were so much lighter in color, and his bare feet hanging there, toes pointing toward the ground. It looked as though someone had taken his boots.

Maurice heard Ruben Vega saying, "He told me, he said they'd bring him to the ranch," the Mexican not protesting but speaking very quietly. "He said they'd hold him there and take a picture, see, to prove he was being held and was unharmed."

C.S. Fly was busy setting up his camera in the road, tilting the box upward, then getting down behind it to look, then adjusting it a little more. C.S. Fly didn't say a word.

"That's what he told me," Ruben Vega said. "They would hold him there and threaten to kill him, yes, if his people didn't move away somewhere else. But he never said he would do this. Never."

Was he telling them something or talking to himself?, Maurice Dumas wondered.

Yes, it sounded more like he was trying to convince himself.

Was it an act, though, for their benefit?

No – listening to the Mexican's tone more than the actual words, Maurice Dumas believed the man was honestly surprised and telling the truth.

Chapter IX

1

The news reporters hanging around the Congress Hotel and the Gold Dollar woke up in a hurry.

A man had been lynched in the middle of the afternoon and that goddamn kid from the *Chicago Times* had scooped them again. (The squirt was even wearing his cap cocked over more on the side of his head.)

Things were happening. C.S. Fly developed three pictures of Armando hanging from the pole like a sack of dirty laundry, made a "showing" of them in his gallery window, marched off to the telegraph office and wired Sheriff John Slaughter in Tombstone; notice, bypassing Deputy R.J. Bruckner.

Why? Because Bruckner was a company

173

stooge and John Slaughter and C.S. Fly were friends, the newsmen speculated. Also to show the mine company that if he, Fly, ran for sheriff of Cochise County next year he was not going to place himself in the company's pocket.

Good stuff was developing. A lot of angles.

Item: Sweetmary was a company town. Without LaSalle Mining there would be no Sweetmary. Therefore the people of Sweetmary and its law enforcement agency would never testify against the company or do anything to put the company in legal jeopardy.

Item: John Slaughter wanted to serve out his term and return to ranching. It was said he was more than willing to use his political weight to help Fly get the Republican nomination. John Slaughter was not a company ass kisser, but he had been in office long enough to have become a realist. Since he was getting out anyway, what did he care what happened here in Sweetmary?

The reporters weren't finished writing that one when John Slaughter arrived in town with a gripsack full of warrants and subpoenas and informed the press that a circuit court judge and county attorney were on their way.

Theory: He was going through the motions to show his friend C.S. Fly the facts of life, liberty and the pursuit of justice in a mine company town.

174

Well, at least they were making a pretty good show of it.

Item: A warrant was issued for the arrest of Phil Sundeen (not even in town a week) and a Mexican by the name of Ruben Vega (Who?). Sundeen was served, arrested and escorted to jail without incident.

Vandozen, the company vice president, was seen in town for a few hours, then was gone — off in a closed carriage to Benson and the Southern Pacific Railroad depot. But a lawyer who had arrived from Bisbee remained. That same day Sundeen posted a five-hundred-dollar bond and was released. The Mexican, Ruben Vega, could not be located.

Items:

C.S. Fly and the squirt from the *Chicago Times*, Maurice Dumas, were subpoenaed as witnesses.

Eladio Duro, Armando's son, appeared in town out of nowhere, riding a burro, and was taken into "protective custody" by John Slaughter.

Bruckner wandered around town and up to the mine works with sixteen John Doe warrants for arrest of the members of Sundeen's security force. He returned with the same number of warrants saying they were nowhere to be found and that they had been discharged

175

from the company payroll.

Bruckner did bring in four dead men, their Sunday suits tearing at the seams, their bodies were so swollen. Three had come from Armando's yard, another from not far away. But only two were identified from personal effects: a man named Wade Miller from Illinois and a man named Henry Shell from Kentucky. Holding his nose as he looked at the other two, Phil Sundeen said no, he did not know their names or was even sure now, because of their bloated condition, he had ever seen them before.

The reporters wanted to know: Well, why the hell didn't they ask Sundeen where the *rest* of his men were?

John Slaughter said he did, and Sundeen had answered: "Who, them? They did not like horseback riding and quit."

Well, did he try to get the truth out of Sundeen?

"You mean by the use of physical force?" John Slaughter asked the reporters. "That is not allowed in the interrogation of suspects. At least not in this county."

But had he used force or not?

Maurice Dumas wrapped a five-dollar bill around a bottle of Green River and put it on R.J. Bruckner's desk as he sat down in the deputy's

176

office. Bruckner did not leave it there more than a moment, getting it into a drawer as Maurice was saying, "Civil servants, I've found, work hard and get little appreciation for their efforts."

"What do you want?" asked Bruckner.

"Haven't you used force on Sundeen to make him talk?"

"Make him talk about what?"

"Where his men are."

"What men? Who saw him with any men?"

"I did," Maurice said.

"Who saw him or any men out where the Mex was found?"

"I saw them here in town."

"So what did you see? Nothing. Get your smart-aleck ass out of here, sonny."

"Who else have you got as a witness," Maurice said, showing his tenacity, "besides Armando's son. Any of the other Mexicans?"

"What Mexicans?"

"Armando's people — the ones that live up there."

"They're gone," Bruckner said, "disappeared. It's you and Fly and the Mex's kid . . . and the Indian agent, Moon."

This surprised Maurice. "You subpoenaed Moon? How come?"

"We believe he saw things."

"Sundeen told you that?"

177

"We know, that's all."

"Has he come to town?"

"He had better be here tomorrow for the hearing. He's not, I'll go and get him. I may be going for him later on anyway."

"Why? For what?"

"Get your smart-aleck ass out of here," Bruckner said. "Time's up."

Item: The circuit court hearing — to determine if a murder had been committed and if there was sufficient reason to believe Sundeen did it — would be held on the second floor of the city jail. The cells up there had not been occupied in several years. Sections of iron bars had been removed and transported to the mine works to be used, it was said, in the construction of a storage facility for high explosives and blasting equipment. Chairs and benches from the Masonic hall and a funeral parlor were now being placed in the second-floor courtroom for the comfort of spectators and visiting newsmen.

Judge Miller Hough of Tombstone was occupying the LaSalle Suite at the Congress Hotel. Prosecutor Stuart "Stu" Ison, who had practiced law in Sweetmary until winning the county position three years ago, was staying with friends.

The services of a young attorney by the name of Goldwater — said to be a nephew of the owner of the well-known Goldwater & Cateñeda General Store in Bisbee — had been retained to act as counsel for Phil Sundeen.

Color item: the mine and crushing mill continued to work two shifts, business as usual, as the town of Sweetmary bustled with activity in preparation for the Hearing. The miners who came down the hill in their coarse work clothes seemed from another world. Many of them were, until recently, from Old World countries. Strange accents and foreign languages were not uncommon on the streets of this mining community.

The news reporters knew what their editors were going to say. Dandy . . . but, goddamn it, where was the Early-Moon confrontation stuff? The stage was set, the suspense built. Now a cattle rustler and ex-con by the name of Sundeen comes along and steals the spotlight. Did he lynch the Mexican or not? What did company-man Bren Early think about it? More important, what were Early and Moon up to during all this, squaring off or just looking at each other?

That was the trouble, they weren't doing anything. But how did you tell an editor Bren Early was holed up at Mrs. Pierson's, wouldn't answer the door, and Moon hadn't showed up yet? If, in fact, he ever would. The newsmen sent wires to their editors that said, in essence, "Big story to break soon," and had a few more drinks while they waited for something to happen.

2

The morning of the hearing the newsmen staying at the Congress came down to the dining room and there was Dana Moon and his wife having breakfast of grits and ham. Moon did not understand what the newsmen were so excited about. Where had he *been?* Home. If they wanted to see him why didn't they come visit? They asked him why he had been subpoenaed and he said that's why they had come to town this morning, to find out.

Moon and his wife, news reporters trailing behind, stopped by the Fly Gallery to see the latest "showing" in the window: Armando hanging from the telegraph pole. Neither of them said anything as they continued down LaSalle Street to the jail and went upstairs to the hearing.

When the reporters who had been waiting outside Mrs. Pierson's house arrived, they said it didn't look like Bren Early was coming.

After all the excitement and suspense the hearing did not prove to be much of a show. (Which

John Slaughter and others could have predicted from the beginning.) Though there was one surprise that stirred considerable interest.

Maurice Dumas, cap under his arm, took the witness stand and told the county attorney, yes, he had seen Mr. Sundeen ride out of Sweetmary with seventeen men. No, Mr. Sundeen would not let any of the reporters follow them. Five hours later he had joined Mr. C.S. Fly and a man in Mr. Sundeen's employ, one Ruben Vega, and accompanied them out to a place where they were to witness a meeting between Mr. Sundeen and Armando Duro. What they found instead was Armando hanging from a pole. Maurice Dumas began to tell about Ruben Vega being "genuinely astonished," but the county attorney, Stuart Ison, said that was all and for him to step down.

C.S. Fly supported the young newsman's testimony as to the purpose of their journey and what they found out on the road. He did not however — if he had witnessed it — mention Ruben Vega's stunned surprise.

Next, Eladio Duro took the stand. Answering the county attorney's questions he admitted, yes, his people had fired on Mr. Sundeen's group when they crossed the property line. (There were several objections by Mr. Goldwater, Sundeen's counsel, during Eladio's testimony, most of which were sustained by Judge Hough.) Eladio described men coming to their house and a Mexican convincing them it was safe to come out to speak to Mr. Sundeen. But as soon as they were outside, Sundeen's men drew pistols and began to shoot at them. Three people fell dead and another was wounded. Before his father could get back in the house Sundeen's men grabbed him and carried him off. Eladio was asked where his family and friends were now. He said they were hiding because they were afraid for their lives. (Objection: judgemental. Sustained.)

Mr. Goldwater, the defense attorney, cross-examined, asking Eladio if the Mexican who spoke to them first carried something in his hands. Yes, Eladio said, a flag of truce. He was asked if his people had fired weapons at Mr. Sundeen and his men. No. But weren't shots fired at Mr. Sundeen's men? No. From others not standing in the yard? Oh, yes; from Sundeen's men who were up on the slope above the house. But weren't three of Sundeen's men struck down by gunfire and killed? Yes, Eladio said. Shot by mistake, he assumed, by their own companions. Eladio was asked to think very carefully before answering the next question. Did the first shots come from the men in the yard or the men on the slope above the house? Eladio was silent and then said, they seemed to both come at the same time.

Mr. Goldwater then called Dana Moon to the stand and asked him if he had been present at Armando Duro's the morning of May the 19th.

"Not actually present," Moon said, already uncomfortable sitting here in this hot room full of people . . . picturing where the cells had been a few years before and where he had talked to Ben through the iron bars.

"But you observed what took place there?"

"Yes."

"You observed a man holding a white flag?"

"Yes."

"How far away were you?"

"About four hundred yards."

"Did you see any others, or another group of men, up on the slope above the house?"

"No."

"You observed the shooting?"

"Yes."

"Did you take part in the shooting?"

"Yes."

"Did you hit anyone?"

Moon hesitated. "I can't say for sure."

"Did you shoot to kill?"

"I fired to prevent Armando and his people, all of them unarmed, from being shot down in cold blood."

183

"Did you shoot to kill?"

"Yes."

Goldwater walked back to the table where Sundeen sat patiently listening before asking Moon, "Did anyone shoot at you?"

"I can't say."

"You mean you can't tell when someone is shooting at you?"

"If they did, they didn't come close."

"You were firing at . . . whom?"

Moon looked at Sundeen three strides away, closer than he had been the last time, in Sonora. Sundeen stared back at him as if ready to smile.

"Him," Moon said, "and his men. They were about . . . they were shooting at Armando's people."

"They were what?"

"I said they were shooting at Armando's people."

"But you fired at them first, didn't you?"

"They were drawing their weapons — at that distance . . . I would say they fired first or at the same time."

"You heard gunfire before you aimed and fired?"

Jesus Christ, Moon thought, feeling the perspiration under his shirt. He said, "I anticipated their fire. Their weapons were out. In a moment they were firing."

"You just said they were drawing their weapons."

"They were drawing — seeing it from that distance, weapons were out. In a moment they were firing."

"What does the distance have to do with it? You saw what you *thought* they intended to do and you reacted, didn't you? You began shooting."

"I knew what they were gonna do. What they *did*. They killed three of the Mexicans, didn't they?"

"I don't know," Mr. Goldwater said. "Did they? There was gunfire coming from two directions. Didn't you open fire first? . . ."

"No, they did."

"And they returned your fire?"

"That wasn't what happened."

"Well, from the facts we have, I would say there was either a grave misunderstanding — the two parties in the yard began to talk and you misinterpreted it, or . . . you deliberately fired at the yard, not caring who you hit, one group or the other. *Or* . . . and this is conjecture, though possibly worth investigating . . . you were purposely firing at the Mexican group —"

"Why would I do that?"

"You realize you admit you fired with intent to kill," the defense lawyer said. "That action is subject to interpretation, for I would dare to say the yard itself was a small target at four hundred yards, where the variance of a fraction of an inch could mean the difference in the taking of one man's life or another man's."

Moon looked at the county lawyer who was not objecting to any of these ideas the defense lawyer was planting. Moon said, "Sundeen was in the yard. Let's hear him tell what happened. It ought to be a pretty good story."

He saw Kate smile and heard sounds of approval from the audience.

But then the defense lawyer stepped in front of him, close, and said quietly, "I could ask who else was up there with you. Do you want to implicate others? Did they also shoot to kill?" The defense lawyer stared at him before adding, "Do you see where I can take this?" Moon felt relief when the dark-haired, well-dressed man from Bisbee turned to Judge Hough and said something and the judge asked Ison, the county lawyer, to approach the bench — the table next to which Moon sat in a straight chair.

Moon heard Goldwater say, "So far there is not one bit of evidence to support a murder charge against my client. No one here can place him with Armando at the scene of the hanging. However, your honor, if you are not reasonably convinced I'll put my client on the stand. He'll testify that he did, in fact, rescue Armando, not carry him off, and left him out there when he said he wanted to return to his people." The judge asked how could the court be certain that was what happened? The defense lawyer asked, who could dispute it?

Moon cleared his throat and almost said, "I can," at this point. He could tell them how he had watched from the high ground as the Mexicans put their dead over horses and rode out of there — maybe to somebody else's place or to hide in the timber — and Armando had not returned as long as they watched. But he couldn't tell them if they didn't ask, and it didn't look like that was going to happen. He tugged at the county lawyer's coat a couple of times, but Ison would not pay any attention to him. Ison had his head stuck in there with the other two legal minds as they talked lawyer talk to each other and decided the outcome of these proceedings.

During the conference at the bench the people in the audience had begun to compare ideas and opinions and there was a buzz of noise in the low-ceilinged courtroom. It stopped when Judge Hough banged his gavel on the desk.

He said that based on a reasonable doubt because of a lack of substantial evidence the charge of suspicion of murder was hereby dismissed.

That was it. The judge left the courtroom and the news reporters converged on Moon and Sundeen: one group asking Moon if he had actually intended to kill Sundeen; another group asking Sundeen what he intended to do about it. Moon said, you heard my testimony. He was looking for the county lawyer, Ison, to tell the little ass-kisser a few things, but did not see him now. Moon felt himself being moved by the crowd clearing away from between them so that finally they stood facing each other.

Sundeen said, "Well, that's twice you have tried. Four hundred yards, huh?"

"Give or take a few," Moon said. "I see you got a hole in your face from the first time and a piece of ear missing."

The reporters were writing in their note pads now — the story unfolding before their eyes, better than they could have staged it, some of them not noticing Sundeen's hand going to his beard to stroke it gently as he stared at Moon.

"You hung a friend of mine and it doesn't look like the court is gonna do anything about it," Moon said.

Sundeen continued to stare at him. He said then, "Go on home. We'll get her done before too long."

"I suppose," Moon said.

One of the reporters said, "Get your guns and

settle it now, why don't you? Out on the street."

Sundeen gave the man a hard stare and said, "For you, you little pissant? Who in the hell do you think you are?"

Moon and Sundeen looked at each other again, each knowing something these reporters would never in their lives understand.

Maurice Dumas waited in front of the jail, watching the people coming out. When he saw Moon and his good-looking young wife, Maurice had to push his way through the crowd to get close enough to hand Moon the folded piece of note paper. Moon looked at Maurice Dumas, nodded hello, then opened the note and read it while the reporters waited. Moon nodded to Maurice again and handed the note to his wife.

"From Bren," he said.

Chapter X

1

Janet Pierson felt left out. She was at ease with them, she liked them; but she didn't feel *with* them. Nor did she feel as close to Bren now. Bren and Dana Moon and his wife had shared something, had lived through an experience during another time that did not include her.

She was aware of the news reporters waiting outside the house, the crowd of them that had followed Moon and his wife here. She liked his wife, Kate; she felt she had known her a long time and the feeling surprised her. For some reason she could sympathize with her; though the young woman did not seem to need or want it. She could also sympathize with the news reporters and knew what they were feeling. She imagined — after Bren and Mr. and Mrs.

190

Moon were gone – the reporters standing at the door asking her questions. What are they like? What did you talk about?

She imagined herself saying, Oh, they're very fine people. Polite, well-mannered.

But what did they talk about?

Nothing in particular. Old times mostly.

Did they get in a fight over the situation?

No, they're friends.

Come on, did they have words?

No. (Not exactly.)

Did they talk about any of the men they'd killed?

No, of course not.

Do you know how many those two have laid to rest?

They would get onto something like that and she would try to close the door.

Did Moon chew tobacco in the house?

Certainly not.

We hear his wife is a tough customer.

She's very nice.

Did she have anything to say?

Of course. She is not timid. She told me about their house.

Was there much tension between them, Early and Moon?

No, it was a very pleasant visit. Mr. Moon described his duties as an Indian agent.

("Through the office of Indian Affairs . . . handle all relations between the federal government and the Indians . . . direct the administration of tribal resources . . . supervise their 'trust' property . . . promote their health and physical welfare . . . guide their activities toward the attainment of economic self-sufficiency, self-government and the preservation of Indian cultural values." Bren said, "And what exactly does that mean?" And Moon said, "Try to keep them from doing what is most natural to them, raiding and making war.") While Mr. Early explained his responsibilities with the company. ("You get a big stockholder out here a thousand and some miles from home, what do you think is the first thing he wants to see?" "An Indian," Moon said. "That's the second thing," Bren said. "A whorehouse," Mrs. Moon said. "Correct," Bren said, and they had a good laugh over it.)

What else might be asked? Janet Pierson wondered if her name would appear in a newspaper or in *Harper's Weekly*. "In an interview with Mrs. Pierson, a close friend of the" . . . legendary, celebrated, renowned . . . famous . . . "the well-known figures who are playing important roles in the controversial land war . . ." What? "Mrs. Pierson stated they are very polite, well-mannered people."

She said, "I don't understand it at all. I don't. How can you sit there like it's just another day and completely ignore what's going on?"

Bren put on a concerned frown. "Honey, we're just visiting; catching up's what we're doing. You know it's been over three years?"

"Yes, I know it's been three years. You date everything you talk about," Janet Pierson said. "Sonora in eighty-seven. St. Helen's, some stagecoach station in eighty-nine. The wedding three years ago . . ."

There was a silence. They seemed content to let it go on, patient people, used to quiet; the Moons sitting together on the sofa could be on the porch Kate had described . . . Bren with a leg over the arm of his chair. Coffee cups on the end tables . . . News reporters outside dying of curiosity: Were they at each other's throats or plotting a way to kill Sundeen?

Bren said, you want some more coffee? The Moons said, no, thank you.

Janet Pierson, hands gripping the arms of her chair, said, "Would you like to hear about my past life, my marriage? How I came to live here? My husband, Paul, was a mining engineer. He designed and built the crushing mill up at the works that one day, when he wasn't feeling well and should have stayed in bed — I told him, in your condition you should *not* be

193

walking around that machinery . . ."

Silence again.

Finally Kate Moon said, "Do you want them to talk about the situation? What do you want?"

"These *two* —" Janet Pierson began, almost angrily and had to calm herself. "These two, the heroic figures — some people must believe they're seven feet tall — what are they *doing?*"

"They're resting," Kate Moon said. "Ask them. Dana, what are you doing?"

"Wondering if we shouldn't be going."

"I'm sorry," Janet Pierson said. "I'm the one acting strange. I'm sincerely sorry."

Kate said, "Bren, what are you doing?"

"I don't know," Bren said. "Passing time? It does seem funny sitting here like this."

Moon looked at him. "What are you gonna do?"

Bren frowned again. "What do you mean, what am I gonna do?"

"Your man lynched my man."

"He isn't in any way *my* man."

"You both work for the same company."

"I don't work. I told you that. I draw money for my claims, that's all."

"All right, you're both paid by the same company."

"I don't have anything to do with this situation. What do you expect me to do, quit? You want me to walk out with them still owing me seventy thousand dollars?"

"I'm not your conscience," Moon said. "I'm not telling you what to do."

"You bet you're not."

There was a silence again.

Kate said to Janet Pierson, "You like it better now?"

"Please — I'm sorry," Janet Pierson said. She was; though she did not feel guilt or remorse. She had to hear what they thought, if she was going to understand them.

Bren rose from the chair. "I'm going to the latrine — if it ain't full of newspaper reporters."

"You still call it that?" Moon said.

Janet Pierson said she wanted to fix them something to eat and followed Bren out to the kitchen.

When they were alone, Moon said, "What are we doing here?"

"Be nice," Kate said.

"I am nice," he said. "That's all I'm doing, just sitting here being nice. I wonder what that son of a bitch Ison is doing. Probably having a drink and a good laugh with the judge and that other lawyer in his new suit."

"You knew what was gonna happen," Kate said. "Don't act so surprised."

He patted her hand. "I'm glad you're so sweet

and understanding. I hope Ison and Hough run again next year so I can vote against them, the ass-kissers."

"Well, our old friend Sundeen would've got off anyway," Kate said. "What did they have to convict him with? Nothing."

"Let's go home."

"If's she's fixing something, we should stay."

Moon looked toward the kitchen door. "Do you suppose he's living here with her?"

"It's his house," Kate said. "He either bought it for her, or so he can say he owns a bigger house than yours —"

"Jesus Christ," Moon said.

"I'm not sure which," Kate said. "But she's a nice person, so don't look down your nose at her."

"I'm not looking down my nose."

"I like her," Kate went on. "She's a feeling person, not afraid to tell you what she thinks."

"Or what other people think," Moon said. "You two should get along fine. You can tell us what's on our minds and save us the trouble of talking about it."

"She's worried about Bren; can't you see that?"

"Bren? Christ, nobody's shooting at Bren. He isn't even in it."

"That's what bothers her," Kate said. "He

won't take sides." She looked up and smiled as Janet Pierson came into the sitting room. "We were just talking about you."

"I don't blame you," the woman said.

Kate made a tsk-tsk sound, overdoing it, shaking her head. "Why worry about what people think? You know what you're doing."

"Sometimes I guess I say too much."

"Sure, when you run out of patience," Kate said. "I know what you mean."

Moon's gaze moved from his wife to the woman, wondering what the hell they were talking about. Then looked toward the door at the sound of someone banging on it, three times. There was a pause. Janet Pierson didn't move. Then came three more loud banging sounds, the edge of somebody's fist pounding the wood panel hard enough to shake the door.

When Bren appeared again in the backyard, coming from the outhouse, the reporters on the other side of the fence in the vacant lot called to him, come on, just give us a minute or so. What were you talking about in there? . . . Debating the issues or what? . . . When's Moon going to meet Sundeen?

Then there was some kind of commotion. The reporters by the fence were looking away, moving off, then running from the vacant lot

197

toward the front of the house. Bren went inside. There were onions and peppers on the wooden drain board in the kitchen, a pot of dry beans soaking. He heard the banging on the front door.

Janet Pierson was standing in the middle of the sitting room, saying, "They're not bashful at all, are they?"

Bren walked past her to the door, pulled it open and stopped, surprised, before he said, "What do you want?"

Deputy J.R. Bruckner stood at the door. Looking past Bren at Moon sitting on the sofa, Bruckner said, "Him. I got a warrant for the arrest of one Dana Moon. He can come like a nice fella or kicking and screaming, but either way he's coming."

2

In Benson, Ruben Vega had to find the right church first, St. John the Apostle, then had to lie to the priest to get him to come from the priest house to the church to hear his Confession.

Kneeling at the small window in the darkness of the confessional, Ruben Vega said,

"Bless me, father, for I have sinned. It has been . . . thirty-seven years since my last confession."

The old priest groaned, head lowered, pinching the bridge of his nose with his eyes closed.

"Since then I have fornicated with many women . . . maybe eight hundred. No, not that many, considering my work. Maybe six hundred only."

"Do you mean bad woman or good women?" the priest asked.

"They are all good, Father," Ruben Vega said. "Let me think, I stole about . . . I don't know, twenty-thousand head of beeves, but only in that time maybe fifty horses." He paused for perhaps a full minute.

"Go on."

"I'm thinking."

"Have you committed murder?"

"No."

"All the stealing you've done — you've never killed anyone?"

"Yes, of course, but it was not to commit murder. You understand the distinction? Not to *kill* someone, to take a life; but only to save my own."

The priest was silent, perhaps deciding if he should go further into this question of murder. Finally he said, "Have you made restitution?"

"For what?"

"For all you've stolen. I can't give you absolution unless you make an attempt to repay those you've harmed or injured."

Jesus, Ruben Vega thought. He said, "Look, that's done. I don't steal no more. But I can't pay back twenty thousand cows. How in the name of Christ can I do that? Oh —" He paused. "And I told a lie. I'm not dying. But, listen, man, somebody is going to," Ruben Vega said, his face close to the screen that covered the little window, "if I don't get absolution for my sins."

He had forgotten how difficult they could make it when you wanted to unburden yourself. But now he was a new person, aware of his spurs making a clear, clean ching-ing sound as he walked out of the empty church — leaving thirty-seven years with the old man in the confessional — going to the depot now to buy a ticket on the El Paso & Southwestern, ride to Douglas, cross the border and go home.

He hung around the yards watching the freight cars being switched to different tracks, smelling the coal smoke, hearing the harsh sound of the cars banging together and the wail of the whistle as an eastbound train headed out for Ochoa and the climb through Dragoon Pass. He wanted to remain outside tonight in the fresh air rather than go to a hotel in

Benson; so he camped by the river and watched the young boys laughing and splashing each other, trying to catch minnows. With dark, mosquitoes came. They drove him crazy. Then it began to rain, a light, steady drizzle, and Ruben Vega said to himself: What are you doing here? He bought a bottle of *mescal* and for ten of the sixty dollars in his pockets he spent the night in a whorehouse with a plump, dark-haired girl named Rosa who thought he was very witty and laughed at everything he said when he wasn't being serious. Though some of the wittiest things he said seriously and they passed over her. That was all right. He gave her a dollar tip. In the morning Ruben Vega cashed in his ticket for the El Paso & Southwestern, mounted his horse and rode back toward the Rincon Mountains standing cleanly defined in the sunlight.

3

R.J. Bruckner said, "Look. They give me a warrant signed by Judge Hough for the arrest of Dana Moon. I served it over all kinds of commotion and people trying to argue with me and those newspaper men getting in the way. It took me and four deputies to clear them out and put Moon in detention. Now you got a complaint, go see the judge or the county attorney, it's out of my hands."

"Are you gonna drink that whole bottle yourself?" Sundeen asked.

He reached behind him to close the door, giving them some privacy in the deputy's little office with its coal-oil lamp hanging above the desk.

"I was having a touch before supper," Bruckner said, getting another glass out of his desk and placing it before Sundeen. "Not that it's any of your business."

"I see they all went home," Sundeen said, "the judge, the prosecutor and John Slaughter, leaving you with a mess, haven't they?"

"I'm doing my job," Bruckner said, pouring a short drink for Sundeen and setting the bottle within easy reach. "I don't see there's any mess here."

Sundeen leaned close as if to pick up the glass and swept the desk clean with his hand and arm, sending bottle, glasses and papers flying against the side wall. It brought the deputy's head up with a jerk, eyes staring open at the bearded, bullet-marked face, the man leaning over the desk on his hands, staring back at him.

"Look again," Sundeen said. "Listen when I'm talking to you and keep your hands in sight, else I'll draw iron and lay it across your head."

It was the beginning of a long night for R.J. Bruckner. First this one coming in and saying he wanted Moon released from jail. What? How was he supposed to do that? You think he just set a person free when somebody asked? Sundeen said he was not asking, he was telling him. He wanted Moon, but he was not going to stick a gun through the bars to get him. He wanted Moon out on the street. Bruckner would send him out and he would take care of it from there.

Ah, now that didn't sound too bad.

Except that Bruckner was looking forward to having Moon stay with him awhile. He owed Moon, the son of a bitch, at least a few lumps with a pick handle but had not gotten around to it yet.

Bruckner sat back thinking about it, saying, "Yeah, like he was shot down while trying to escape."

"Jesus, it doesn't take you long, does it?" Sundeen said.

Bruckner did not get that remark. He was thinking that he liked the idea of Moon being shot down even better than taking a pick handle to him . . . especially if it turned out he was the one pulled the trigger and not this company dude with the silver buckles.

"Yeah," he said, nodding, "let me think on it awhile."

Then he was pulled up short again as Sundeen said, "You bag of shit, the thinking's been done. He walks out of here tonight at . . . let's say eleven o'clock, after you show him a release form."

"A release form? I don't have anything like that."

"Jesus, you show him *some*thing. A wire from the county clerk saying the charge's been dropped. Eleven o'clock, open the door for him to walk out and duck," Sundeen said. "You do anything else, like try and back-shoot him, you'll see fireworks go off in your face."

First Sundeen —

Then Bren Early walking into the office, looking at the mess on the floor where the bottle had knocked over the spittoon and the papers lying there were stained with tobacco juice and whiskey.

"Come to see your old partner?"

"In a minute," Early said, looking down at Bruckner from where Sundeen had stood a little while before. "You owe me a favor."

"For what?"

"Not killing you three years ago. That would be reason enough to do what I ask, but I'm gonna give you another one." Early brought paper scrip from his inside coat pocket and dropped it on the desk. "Being practical – why was he arrested in the first place?" Early watched Bruckner pick up the money and begin to count it. "Because he admitted in court trying to shoot somebody. But how're they gonna convict him if he stands mute at his trial? Moon being an agent of the federal government and all –"

"Five hundred," Bruckner said, looking up.

"Since he'd get off anyway – all you'd be doing is cutting a corner, wouldn't you?"

Bruckner folded the money into his shirt pocket and sat back, getting comfortable, big nose glistening in the coal-oil light. "I would need to do a little preparing, make it look real, you understand."

"I was thinking, in a few days when you take him to the county seat," Early said. "Out on the road someplace –"

"No, it's got to be tonight," Bruckner said.

"Why is that?"

"Because I'm on duty tonight and if I'm gonna do this I want to get it done, over with." Bruckner paused. He had to think, picture it,

205

without taking too much time. If Sundeen and Early were both waiting outside . . . If they saw each other as Moon came out . . . If they went for each other, there'd be guns going off, wouldn't there, and he could maybe have a clear shot at Moon going out and then, what if he put the gun on Early, if Early was still standing up? . . . Shoot the accomplice . . . Jesus Christ, shoot Sundeen if he had to, if he saw the chance . . . Shoot all three of them during the confusion . . . Shoot those big names in the newspapers, God Almighty, gun them down, all three of them shot dead by Deputy Sheriff R.J. Bruckner . . . Oh yes, that's Bruckner, he's the one that gunned down Moon, Bren Early and Phil Sundeen, the Yuma terror, during a daring jailbreak . . . Wiped them out, all three of them. Jesus.

"What're you nervous about?" Early asked him.

Bruckner pulled out a handkerchief to wipe his forehead and down over his nose and mouth. "Goddamn dinky office is like a hotbox. I'm gonna get out of here pretty soon, run for the job in Tombstone next year. Shit, if I can't beat Fly, with my experience in law enforcement —"

"Let's get this done first," Early said.

Bruckner nodded, mind made up. "Tonight, eleven o'clock ... No, five minutes before eleven. You come, leave a horse for him in front. Step inside and give me a nod. I'll go back and get your partner, lock myself up in his cell."

"Why not the back door?" Early said. "In the alley."

"That door don't open. It's bolted shut."

"All right, let me talk to him now."

"Tell him five minutes before eleven," Bruckner said.

This time it was Moon in the cell and Early looking through the bars.

He said, "I talked to John Slaughter before they moved their show out of here. John says they didn't have a choice, you shot three men in that yard. They'll hold your trial at the county seat. Now, considering everything, the company'll turn on the pressure to get a conviction. See if they can send you to Yuma."

"It's a lot of country from here to there," Moon said. "Kate visits tomorrow, I'll talk to her about it. You don't have to get involved in this."

"I already am," Early said. "Sundeen was here about a half-hour ago. The way I see it, he doesn't want you in here either. He's been keeping quiet, but that business in Sonora's still eating him."

"I know that," Moon said.

"I talked to Bruckner and he was already there waiting. Had the time set and everything."

"What'd you pay him?"

"Not much. He owes me a favor. But wouldn't it make his heart glad to shoot you going out the door and me standing there? Or Sundeen. He paid a visit — something's already been arranged here, I can feel it."

"I can smell it," Moon said. "But this isn't any of your business. If he's gonna open the door, I'll take my own chances."

"What was it you said the time I was in there and you were out here?" Early paused before reciting the words from three years ago. " 'You might see it coming, but I doubt it.' Well, you'll probably hear me three blocks away."

"Drawing your sword and yelling, 'Charge,' " Moon said. "It should be something to watch."

4

The parlor was semi-dark with only one lamp lit, turned low. When Kate came down the stairs, Janet Pierson turned from the front window.

"Did you rest?"

"A little. I didn't sleep though."

Kate walked over to the hall tree and took down her husband's suitcoat and holstered revolver. (They had taken him out of the house in his shirtsleeves, hurrying to get him past the throng of newsmen.)

Watching her, Janet said, "I envy you. I'm not sure why, but I do."

Kate draped the coat over the back of a chair. Holding the shoulder holster, she slipped the Colt's revolver in and out of the smooth leather groove, then drew the gun and looked at the loads in the chambers as she said, "You don't have to envy anyone. You can do whatever you want with your life."

"But you *know* what you want."

"This minute I do," Kate said. "I want my husband. If I have to shoot somebody to get him, I will. It's not something I have to think about and decide." She looked toward the kitchen, at the sound of the back door opening and closing, then at Janet again. "This doesn't mean anything to you personally. Why get mixed up in something just for the sake of taking sides?"

The question was left unanswered. Bren Early came in from the kitchen with saddlebags over one shoulder.

"I haven't seen a soul in front," Janet said to him.

"Tired of waiting around," Bren said. "They're in the saloon telling each other stories." He took the holstered revolver from Kate and slipped it into the saddlebag that hung in front of him. "I still think it'd be better if you waited here."

Kate shook her head. "I'll be out on the road. If you won't let me any closer —"

"You might hear shooting," Bren said. "This man wants to make it look real. Stay where you are till Moon gets there. But for some reason he doesn't — he gets delayed or has to ride out the other way, you come back here."

"What do you mean, gets delayed? I thought it was all arranged."

"It is. I'm talking about if something happens to change the plan . . . somebody comes along doesn't know about it. That's all."

"You're not telling me everything," Kate said. "What is it?"

"Believe me," Bren said, "Dana's gonna walk out. But you have to be patient and not spook if you hear a lot of noise. All right? Wait'll I'm gone a few minutes before you leave."

"I'll be out there before eleven," Kate said. "By the first bend."

Janet watched Bren pick up Moon's coat, then lean toward Kate and kiss her on the cheek. Turning he looked at Janet. "I'll be back in a little while." And went out through the kitchen.

The room was quiet again.

"I don't know what to say to him." Janet turned to the window to watch for him. He'd ride past the front of the house leading Moon's horse.

"Then don't say anything," Kate said, walking over to her, her gaze going out the window to the dark street.

"I feel — I don't feel part of him or what any of you are doing."

"Well, you can come up the mountain for a visit, except I don't think it's a very good time." Kate paused and put her hand on Janet's shoulder. "Why don't you just marry him and quit thinking about it?"

"You sound like Bren now."

"If you have to be absolutely sure before you make a move," Kate said, "then forget it. Else you're gonna be sitting her with cobwebs all over you."

LaSalle Street was quiet: first-shift miners in bed for the night, the second shift still up at the works where dots of lantern light marked the shaft scaffolding and company buildings; the crushing mill was dark, the ore tailings black humps running down the slope.

Sundeen, mounted, came down out of that darkness into the main street, holding his horse to a walk past the store fronts and evenly spaced young trees planted to grow along the sidewalk. The porch of the Congress Hotel was deserted. Lights showed in the lobby and in saloons and upstairs windows down the street. It was quarter to eleven. At the sound of gunfire they'd pour out of the saloons — most of them who were sober or not betting against a pot — the news reporters coming out of their hangout, the Gold Dollar, which was on the northeast corner of LaSalle and Fourth streets. The jail was on the southwest corner, the cellblock extending along Fourth toward Mill Street. On the corner across Fourth from the jail was the Maricopa State Bank. On the corner across LaSalle — where Sundeen now dropped his reins and stepped down from his horse — was the I.S. Weiss Mercantile Store.

Sundeen, looking at the jail and its two lighted windows – the one to the left of the door Bruckner's office – did not see the dark figure sitting on the steps of the bank, catty-corner from him.

When the figure got to its feet Sundeen caught the movement and knew who it was: yes, crossing Fourth Street toward the jail with something dark draped over his shoulder and carrying a short club or something in his left hand. No, not a club. The object gave off a glint and took shape in the light from the jail window and Sundeen saw it was a stubby little shotgun.

Early stopped. He half turned to look across toward the Mercantile Store.

"It isn't gonna be as easy as you thought."

"What is?" Sundeen said. "Shit."

"Where're all your men at?"

"I didn't think I'd need them this evening."

"Well," Early said, "you better decide if you're gonna be there when we come out."

"God damn Bruckner," Sundeen said. "I think he has got cow shit for brains."

"No, he's not one to put your money on," Early said. "Well, I'll see you if you're still gonna be there." He moved past the jail

213

window toward the front door.

There was nobody to trust, Bruckner had decided. Not a friend, not one of his four deputies. Not in something like this. The chance, if it came, would be there for him alone and he would have to do it himself if he wanted to reap the benefits. And, oh my Lord, the benefits. Both at hand and in the near future, with a saloon-full of news reporters across the street to begin the spread of his fame which would lead to his fortune. All he had to do, at the exact moment when he saw the chance, was pull the trigger three times − at least two times − and in the coming year he would be the Fighting Sheriff of Cochise County . . . working angles the mine company and the taxpayers never knew existed. Being ready was the key. Here is how he would do it:

Early sticks his head in the door, gives him the nod.

Unarmed, he goes back to the lock up, thanking the Lord he had put Moon in a cell by himself.

He steps in, Moon steps out, locks him in. As soon as Moon is through the door, into the front part of the jail . . .

He unlocks the cell with a spare key, goes through to the front, gets the loaded shotgun and Peacemaker from under the cabinet . . .

Runs to the door — maybe hearing Sundeen's gunfire about then — and opens up on them with the shotgun, close behind, while they're busy with Sundeen.

Then, as Sundeen comes across the street — and before anybody is out of the Gold Dollar — blow out Sundeen's lights.

If Sundeen's fire turns them back in the jail, which was possible, he'd bust them as they came though the door. Then step out and shoot Sundeen with the Peacemaker, saying later the man had fired at him after he'd told him to drop his gun, so he'd had no choice but to return fire. (He could hear himself telling it, saying something about being sworn to enforce the law, by God, no matter who the armed men were he had to face.) Killing the two should buy him the ticket to the county seat; but he would like to notch up Sundeen also, long as he was at it.

In case of an unexpected turn — if he somehow lost his weapons and found himself at close quarters, he had a two-shot bellygun under his vest, pressing into his vitals.

At a quarter to eleven Bruckner stopped pacing around the front room of the jail, moving from the railing that divided the room to the front window and back, went into his office and sat down, wishing he had just a couple swallows of that Green River drying on the floor.

At five to eleven he thought he heard voices outside. He turned to the window, but came around again as he heard the door open and close. Bren Early appeared in the doorway to his office wearing his .44's, saddlebags over his shoulder and carrying a sawed-off shotgun. At this moment Bruckner's plan began to go all to hell.

"O.K.," Bruckner said, geting up and coming out to the front room as Early stepped back. "You got his horse?"

Early nodded.

"I'll fetch him. Go on outside."

Early looked at Bruckner's empty holster, then over at the gun rack, locked with two vertical iron bars. "Where the keys?"

"Don't worry — go on outside." Bruckner took a ring of keys from the desk in the front room, walked to the metal-ribbed door leading to the cell block and unlocked it before looking back at Early.

"What're you waiting on?"

Early moved toward him, making a motion with the sawed-off shotgun.

Early coming back with him wasn't in the plan. But maybe it wouldn't hurt anything. It could even make it easier, having the two right together.

Bruckner glanced over his shoulder walking down the row of cells. He raised his hands as one of the prisoners, then another, saw them and pushed up from their bunks. A voice behind Early said, "Hey, partner, open this one. Let me out of this shit hole."

Moon stood at his cell door. He stepped aside as Bruckner entered, made a half-turn and came around to slam a fist into the side of Bruckner's face. The deputy hit the adobe wall and slid to the floor. Moon stood over him a moment, seeing blood coming out of the man's nose. He said, "Don't ever put your hands on me again," and gave him a parting boot in the ribs, drawing a sharp gasp from Bruckner.

Early held the lockup door open as Moon came through, then slammed it closed, cutting off the voices of the prisoners yelling to be let out.

"Sundeen was out in front. Just him I could see, but it doesn't mean he's alone," Early said.

From the saddlebags Moon took his folded-up coat and shoulder rig and slipped them on, saying, "How far you going in this?"

"See you get out here, that's all. But

217

Sundeen's a different matter. I mean if he wants to try." Early paused. "If he doesn't, maybe we should go find him, get the matter settled."

Moon was smoothing his coat, adjusting the fit of the holster beneath his left arm. He took the sawed-off from Early. "I ain't lost any sleep over him. Least I haven't yet."

"No, but he's gonna bother you now, he gets the chance. I'd just as soon finish it."

Moon seemed to study him, forming words in his mind. "Is it you've been sitting around too long, you're itchy? Or you just want to shoot somebody?"

"I can go home and leave it up to you," Early said, a cold edge there.

"Yes, you can. And I'd probably handle him one way or the other."

Early stared at Moon a moment, turned and walked toward the door.

Moon said, "You understand what I mean? I want to be sure about him."

Early pulled the door wide open and stepped aside. "Go on and find out then." Still with the cold edge.

Shit, Moon thought. He said, "Get over your touchiness. You sound like a woman." And walked out the door past him — the hell with it — out in the middle of the street, looking

218

around, before he saw his horse over by the side of the bank. He didn't see any sign of Sundeen and didn't expect to; the man wasn't going to shoot out of the dark and not get stand-up credit for his kill.

Early came out to the board sidewalk, pulling the door partly closed behind him. He said, "Go on home, sit on your porch. Kate's waiting up by the bend."

"Thanks," Moon said, glancing over, already moving toward Fourth Street.

"You don't have to thank me for anything," Early said. "We're even now, right? Don't owe each other a thing."

Jesus, Moon thought. He should hear himself.

He saw the light in the half-closed doorway behind Early widen. He saw a figure, Bruckner, and yelled, "Bren!" and had to drop the sawed-off with Bren in the way and the door too far; he had to drop it to pull the goddamn saddlebags off his shoulder and come out with the Colt's, seeing Early throwing himself out of the way as Bruckner's shotgun exploded and Moon's revolver kicked in his hand and he saw Bruckner punched off his feet as the .44 took him somewhere in the middle of the body. Bren was up then, yelling at him to go on, get out of here, waving his arm.

You better, Moon thought, picking up the sawed-off. He could see Bruckner's feet in the doorway, beyond Early. And sounds now from across the street, people starting to come out of the Gold Dollar, standing there, looking this way. Moon reached his horse and stepped up; he pointed toward Mill Street and was gone in the darkness.

Chapter XI

1

Moon stopped at White Tanks on the way home "to put in an appearance," he told Kate, say hello to the reservation Apaches he hadn't seen in weeks and sort through his mail — any directives, bulletins or other bull shit he might have received from Washington.

Kate said she was glad she didn't have to read it. She would go home and light the fire. He watched her take off across the pasture toward the brushy slope and start up the switchback trail that climbed through the field of saguaro, watching her until she was a tiny speck, his little wife up there on the mountain, and said to himself, "You know how lucky you are?" He was anxious to get home to her. Maybe he'd look at the mail but check on the reservation people tomorrow.

He sat down at his desk though, to read the letter from the Bureau of Indian Affairs, Interior Department, Washington, D.C. It took him about a quarter of an hour to find out all the two and a half pages of official language actually said was, he was fired . . . would be relieved of his duties for disregarding such and such, as of a date three months from now. Fired because he hadn't brought his Indians down off the mountain, failing to comply with directive number . . . some long number. The fools. They could have said it in two words.

He'd go home and tell Kate and watch her eyes open — Kate poised there, not knowing whether to show relief or rail at the imbeciles in the bureau, pausing and then asking, "Well, how do you feel about it?"

How did he feel?

Relief, yes, able to wade out of the official muck, walk off. Or would he be walking *out*, leaving the reservation people when they needed him? Well, they may need *some*body, but he wasn't doing them a hell of a lot of good, was he? And what difference did it make now, since he didn't have a choice but to leave? Thinking about all that at once, blaming himself for not having thought of an answer sooner . . . and hearing the bootsteps on the porch, the ching-ing sound, without first hearing a horse approach —

The Mexican stood in the open doorway. The one from Sonora. The one from Duro's yard with the white flag. Hesitant. Raising his hands from his sides.

"You didn't walk here," Moon said.

"I didn't want to startle you. Maybe you come out shooting you hear me," Ruben Vega said. "Listen to me and believe it, all right? I don't work for Sundeen no more, but he's up on the mountain."

"Where?" Moon came out of his swivel chair.

"Going to your house."

"When was this?"

"Last night, very late."

Moon came around his desk and Ruben Vega had to get out of his way. He followed Moon out to the porch.

"Wait. I want to tell you something. I didn't *see* him up there, I heard it, where he's going."

Moon, at his horse gathering the reins, looked up at the Mexican. "Tell it quick."

"See, I quit him. I went to Benson. I was going to go home, but I decide after all the years, after all the bad things I done —"

Moon stepped up into his saddle.

"I came back here to do some good, be on the good side for a change — whether you believe

223

me or not." He saw Moon's look. "Listen to me, all right? I came back, I stop by this place where I believe his men have been waiting. The J-L-Bar, an old, worn-out place. Yes, there they are. They say, where you been? Listen —"

Moon was reining, moving out.

"They say to me Sundeen comes tonight and we go up the mountain to get the man name Moon. You hear me?" Shouting it.

Ruben Vega ran to his horse ground-tied in the pasture. Maybe he would catch up to Moon already racing for the brush slope, maybe he wouldn't.

She'd say to him, "Come to bed." He'd say, "It's daytime." She'd say, "I mean to *sleep*," after riding most the night — God, she had been glad to see him coming out the road with the lights of Sweetmary behind him. She wanted at least to hug and kiss him awhile, touch him, make sure he was here.

Kate built a fire in the stove and put on a pot of coffee before going outside again to tend Goldie. She led the palomino around the house to the corral that was made of upright mesquite poles wired together. This pen was attached to a timber and thatched-roof structure open at both ends that served as a horse barn. Kate heard the sound — a horse hoof on gravel . . . a soft whinny . . . then silence — as she was leading Goldie across the corral.

She looked through the barn to the back of the property where open graze reached to a brush thicket and a tumble of boulders. There the ground began to climb again. An Apache could be passing by. Even when Moon said they were close she rarely saw one, unless they were coming out and wanted to be seen. They kept to themselves. Red, the little bow-legged chief, was the only one she had ever spoken to; the women just grinned when she tried talking to them in Spanish learned from Moon. Yes, it could be an Apache going by. Her gaze raised to the escarpment of seamed rock standing against the sky. Or they might be up there watching over her.

But she had the feeling someone else was much closer. She turned to Goldie, patting her as she moved back to the saddlebags, raised the leather flap close to her face and drew the .38 double-action revolver Moon had given her that time in Sonora and have given to her again in the past month.

Someone was watching her. Not Apaches, someone else.

Kate led Goldie back to the mesquite-pole gate, dragged it open enough to let them through. As she prepared to mount — looking over the saddle and through the open-ended barn again, she saw the four riders coming out of the brush thicket, walking their horses, looking right at her. Kate stepped into the saddle kicking, turning the corner to the front of the house and reined in, not knowing what to do, Goldie sidestepping, nervous, feeling Kate's heels and the reins and, between the two, Kate's indecision.

Sundeen sat his mount with two riders near. A bunch more were by the adobe wall and coming through the gate on foot, all of them holding rifles.

"Well, it's been a long time," Kate said, resigned.

"What?" Sundeen studied her, not knowing what she meant.

"You don't remember, do you?"

Sundeen, squinting now, shook his head.

"One time, I was twelve years old playing by the river," Kate said. "You come along, tried to pull my britches down and I smacked you with a rock."

"Jesus Christ," Sundeen said, "down Lanoria."

"You were grown then, too, you dirty pervert."

"Yeah, I believe I recall that — hit me with a big goddamn rock." He looked at one of his

226

riders who was wearing a vest and derby hat. "Thing musta weighed five pounds. Hit me square on the forehead with it." Sundeen nudged his horse forward. "So you're the one, huh? You should've give in that time and seen the elephant at an early age." Still coming toward her. "Or I could give you another chance while we're waiting around." He pulled in then. "Hey now — but you better throw that gun down first."

Kate raised the .38 from her lap. "Or I could put a hole in the other side of your face, match the one you already got."

"Sweetheart," Sundeen said, "before you could aim that parlor gun I'd have sent you off to the angels. Now let it fall."

Of course, the man was thinking of his wife. Ruben Vega realized this. He should have realized also — knowing something about Moon — the man would control his emotion and not ride blindly up the ravine to be shot from his saddle. So Ruben Vega was able to catch up with the man once they were in the high rocks, somewhere north of the ravine, perhaps on an approach to the side or back of the house; Ruben Vega wasn't exactly sure where they were when he reached Moon. Or when the Apache appeared ahead of them, waiting in the trail. One moment the steep terrain ahead empty, the next moment the dark little half-naked man standing there with a carbine and a cartridge belt around his skirt. A headband of dark wool, as dark as his dark-leather face; he could be an old man, or any age.

The Apache, Red, motioned and went off through the towering outcropping of rocks, through a seam that became a trail when they dismounted and followed, winding, climbing through the rock and brush until the trail opened and the entire sky seemed to be close above them, a very clear soft blue. A beautiful day to feel good and be alive, the Mexican was thinking. Except for the situation, the man's wife — Moon and the Apache, and now three more Apaches who had appeared from no-where, were looking down the wall of rock . . . as though from the top of a church steeple, the Mexican thought, seeing the stone side of the house below, the thatched roof of a barn, a corral, riders in the front yard . . . the glint of the woman's blonde hair in the sunlight close to Sundeen . . . Yes, it was Sundeen and two others . . . four more coming from the corral side of the house . . . the rest of them out by the adobe wall, watching the approach from the ravine.

A good day, the Mexican thought, feeling alive and yet calm inside. A day he would mark in his mind, whatever the date was. He would find it out later.

He said to Moon, "Is there a way down from here?"

Moon looked at him. The man could skip all the questions in his mind and trust him or not.

Moon said, "You go down . . . then what?"

The man was open. He had nothing to lose by listening.

"You stay behind me, out of sight," Ruben Vega said. "Come in close as you can when I talk to him."

"Tell him what?"

"I don't know. What comes in my mind. He'll be curious a few minutes — where have you been, partner? All that. Then you have to be close. I can talk to him some more, but it comes out the same in the end, uh? He isn't going to say to your wife, go on, stay out of the way. So —" the Mexican shrugged.

"Thirteen of them," Moon said.

"More than that last night at the J-L-Bar. He hired some more maybe he send someplace else, I don't know." Moon was staring at him again and Ruben Vega said, "I never done this before, but it's a good day to begin. Now,

229

how do you get down from here?"

There were ten at the adobe wall now, dismounted. One with a derby hat sat his horse in the middle of the yard, a Winchester across his lap, squinting up at the high rocks. One on the porch was holding a coffee pot. Sundeen, still mounted, was gazing about, looking up at the rocks trying to see something, nervous or not sure with that high ground above him. Moon's wife was still on the palomino: as though Sundeen hadn't made up his mind yet, keep her here or take her somewhere, or trying to think of a way to use her.

Good, Ruben Vega thought, approaching the yard from the corral side of the house, almost to the yard before they saw him. Very good.

"I think you need me," the Mexican said, "for eyes. Man, I ride up, you don't even see me."

Sundeen gave him a patient look, shaking his head. "Where the hell you been?"

"I went to Benson to go to church," Ruben Vega said.

"Yeah, I know, piss all your money away and come back for some more, haven't you? Well, make yourself useful, partner. Ride on down a ways and see if he's coming."

"I already did," Ruben Vega said. "He's coming up pretty soon, over there," pointing to the wall where the shooters were waiting with their rifles, not wearing their suitcoats now, several of them with straw hats pulled down low.

The one in the derby hat rode over that way and Sundeen sat for some moments twisted around in his saddle, looking toward the wall.

Now, the Mexican thought, right hand on his thigh, inches from his revolver.

But he couldn't do it and the next moment it was too late. Sundeen was turning back to him.

Ruben Vega looked away. He saw the revolver on the ground next to the palomino. Moon's wife sat still, though her eyes moved and she listened. Of course, she listened. He wished he could tell her something: Be ready. Be watching me.

"Alone?"

"What?" the Mexican said.

"Was he alone?"

"Yes. Maybe they can see him now," the Mexican said and looked toward the wall again.

But Sundeen didn't turn this time and the Mexican had a strange feeling of relief, not having to decide in that moment to pull his gun . . . not wanting to shoot the man from a blind side, but not wanting to die either. So how was he supposed to do it? Thirty-seven years doing this, carrying a gun since he was fourteen years old, not worrying before about killing a man if he believed the man might kill him first. Why was he thinking about it now? Because he was getting old. Sundeen would say to him, you're getting old; and he would say, yes, because I'm still alive. It was a beautiful day and if it was going to be the one he'd remember he'd better do it now. Without thinking anymore.

But he thought of one more thing.

He said, "I'm taking the woman."

Alerting her with his words.

But alerting Sundeen also — seeing his expression only for a moment puzzled.

His hand going to his holster, to the hard grip of the .44, the Mexican saw Sundeen's hand moving, and knew he shouldn't have said anything and now was going to lose . . . But the woman was moving, kicking her palomino around . . . as Sundeen's revolver cleared and he was firing and firing again . . . and, Christ, it was like being punched hard, hearing himself grunt with the wind going out of him and the .44 in his hand, trying to put it on Sundeen . . . *ughhh*, grunting again in the noise of something hard socking him in the chest . . . firing as he saw the blue sky and felt himself

232

going back, falling—

Sundeen had several thoughts in the next moments:

That was a good horse, Ruben's, not to have moved under all that commotion, the horse standing there, his old segundo gone crazy and now dead on the ground.

Everybody back there see it? It was time he showed them something.

Three snap shots dead center. Any *one* would have killed the crazy Mexican.

Three shots. Two left in his Peacemaker — that thought hitting him all at once as he saw the movement, as he saw the Apaches first, *Apaches*, a bunch of them off in the scrub, and Moon appearing at the corner of the house, Moon yelling his wife's name. Moon blocked out for a moment as the palomino shot past him —the woman's blonde hair in the horse's blonde mane. Sundeen extended his Peacemaker and fired, saw Moon again, there he was, and tried to concentrate his aim on Moon with one load left — and the heavy fire came all at once from the scrub. Sundeen fired at Moon suddenly moving — shit — yanked his reins to get out of there, yelling, "Get 'em, goddamn it . . . get 'em!"

Moon wanted him so bad, putting his Colt's

gun on the man tight-reining, kicking his horse, at the same time, seeing the ones way over by the wall raising their rifles, opening fire, and thinking, *Kate,* looking to see where she was — there, past him, still low in her saddle and cutting through the scrub to come around by the corral behind him. In that moment of concern letting Sundeen get the jump he needed, Sundeen beating his mount toward the shooters by the wall. Moon aimed stiff-armed, ignoring the shooters, pulling the trigger five times, holding the sawed-off in his left hand and wishing he had the Sharps for just one, take his time and *right then,* blow out Sundeen's soul as his horse cleared the wall and there he was for a split moment against the sky. But not today.

Now it was Moon's turn to get out of there.

They withdrew to high ground, Moon, his wife and his Apaches, and took careful shots at the figures crouched on the other side of the wall now. The figures would return fire, shooting at puffs of smoke. Ruben Vega's body lay in the yard, his chestnut horse nuzzling him as though it were grazing.

"Keep 'em away from the house," Moon said.

Kate remembered the one on the porch with the coffee pot, the fresh coffee she'd made for her husband, and said there was one already in there.

After awhile heavy black smoke began to pour out of the stone chimney.

"He's burning the place," Kate said. "He's burning our home."

Moon waited in the high rocks with his Sharps rifle, seeing from this angle, the side and back of the house, the clay-tile roof and most of the yard, but not the porch, the front of the house. The thick smoke billowed up from the chimney.

When the smoke began to seep out across the yard from the front, Moon judging it was coming out of the door and windows, he raised the Sharps and pressed his cheek to the smooth stock, the big curled hammer eased back in front of his eyes, the barrel pointing into the yard, and waited.

Finally Kate said, "There he is."

Moon saw the figure appear beyond his front sight, running for the wall. There was a faint sound, the men down there yelling, cheering him on. The figure reached the wall and bounded up to go over it in one motion. Moon paused, seeing the man stop and draw himself up to stand on the wall with hands on his hips and look around at his work . . . the smoke pouring out of the house.

Another fool, Moon thought. He shot the fool cleanly off the wall, the man dying as the heavy sound boomed out into the distance. It was not much satisfaction. After awhile Sundeen and his shooters pulled out.

Moon and Kate went down to their house, beat at the smoldering pockets of fire with blankets and dragged out the charred furniture that had been piled in the middle of the room. When this was done, Moon put the Mexican over his horse. They took him down to the White Tanks cemetery, buried him and recited a prayer over his grave. If they ever learned his name they would put up a marker.

2

R.J. Bruckner showed the news reporters and anyone interested the little derringer that had saved his life. The gun, lying on the deputy's desk, looked like it had been hit with a hammer. Patting his belly, Bruckner said he kept the little pea-shooter right here, see, exactly where Moon's bullet had caught him. The bullet struck the derringer and embedded parts of it into his flesh the doctor had to pull out with tweezers.

Where had Moon got a gun to shoot with?, the newsmen wanted to know.

When his wife had visited, Bruckner said. He

had taken Mrs. Moon's word she had no weapons on her person, so had not searched her.

Maurice Dumas, who was present, asked himself when Moon's wife had visited him in the eight hours Moon was in jail. Maurice thought about it and shook his head. She hadn't.

Bruckner said Moon had pulled the gun and locked him in the cell, not knowing – Bruckner patting his pocket now – he always carried a spare key. He had then grabbed his six-shooter, run out to the street and would have shot Moon dead had not Bren Early gotten in the way, Early having come just then to visit Moon.

The news reporters gave Bruckner narrow looks while some of them laughed out loud, which was a mistake. It shut off Bruckner's trust of them and willingness to talk. After that it was like pulling teeth to get information from him.

Grimly he stuck to his story that it was Moon's wife who'd given him the gun and had brought the horse some of the newsmen had actually seen running down Fourth Street toward Mill with Moon aboard. Yes, in fact Moon had sneered at him and actually *told* him, when he was being locked in the cell, that it was his wife had brought it. Also, he knew for a fact Moon's wife had left, Mrs. Pierson's house about the time of Moon's escape. She was no longer in town, was she? "Now get your asses out of my office."

Bruckner didn't have any need for these grinning, smart-aleck out-of-towners. He had work to do. First thing, post the wanted dodger on Dana Moon. It showed Moon's face, taken from a C.S. Fly photo, and said:

$5,000
REWARD

(Dead or Alive)

for information leading to
the arrest or seizure of

DANA MOON
Escaped Fugitive

37 years of age, dark hair,
dark-complected. Former United States
Government Indian Agent at White Tanks
Sub-agency. Approach with caution. If
whereabouts known, notify Deputy Sheriff
R.J. Bruckner, Sweetmary, Arizona
Territory.

Bruckner hung the dodger outside the jail on a bulletin for all to see. On the same board were: A LaSalle Mining Company notice warning hunters and prospectors to avoid posted areas

238

where survey crews were working with dynamite.

And, a recruiting poster — "HIGH PAY — INTER-ESTING WORK" — calling for individuals who were experienced in the handling of firearms and owned their own horse to apply for a position with the LaSalle Mining Security Division. "$20 A WEEK TO START. SEE P. SUNDEEN."

Maurice Dumas looked at the board for several minutes, the thought striking him, wasn't it strange the company posters were right there with the Moon "wanted" dodger? Like the company was footing the bill for all three enterprises. They surely looked alike in appearance. He could write an article about that, posing the question: Was the company paying for Dana Moon's arrest . . . or death? (Bruckner had refused to answer that directly, saying it was county business.)

But first, locate Early, if possible, and see if he was willing to chat about things in general. Maurice Dumas was still feeling intuitive as well as pretty lucky.

Was it because he had not been pushy, but had politely given his name and said he was sorry to have disturbed her? Maurice couldn't believe it when she said come in. Look at that. The first news reporter to be invited into the house of the mysterious Mrs. Pierson. He entered hesitantly,

239

cap in hand, looking around with an expression of awe, for this place could some day be of historical interest.

She did not invite him to sit down, but immediately said, "You're the one he talks to, aren't you?"

"Well, we have spoken privately several times, yes," Maurice said. "I mean he's told me things he hasn't told the other journalists, that I know of."

"Like what?"

"Well . . . how he feels about things."

"He does? He tells you that, how he feels?"

"I don't mean to imply I have his complete confidence, no, ma'am." He didn't realize until now that she was upset. Judging from her tone, more than a little angry.

"Well, the next time you see him," Janet Pierson said, "tell him to quit acting like a spoiled brat and grow up."

"Mr. *Early?*"

"Like he got out of bed on the wrong side every morning. Tell him to make up his mind what he's mad at. If it's me, if I'm to blame, I'll gladly move out. Ask him if that's what he wants. Because I'm not taking any more of his pouting."

"Bren *Early?*"

"Or his silence. All day he sat here, didn't say a

word. 'Can I get you something? . . . Would you like your dinner now?' Like walking on eggs, being so careful not to bother him too much. He'd grunt something. Did that mean yes or no? He'd grunt something else. Finally I said, 'Well, if you're gonna act as if I'm not here, one of us might as well leave.' No answer. Can you imagine living with someone like that?"

She did not seem too mysterious now.

"Bren Early?" Maurice said, puzzled. "No, I can't imagine him like that. He's so . . . calm. Are you sure he wasn't just being calm?"

"God," Janet Pierson said, "you *don't* know him, do you? You believe the one in the photograph with the revolvers is the real person."

"Well, what I do know about him is certainly real and impressive enough to me," Maurice said.

"It is, huh?" Mrs. Pierson said something then that Maurice thought about for a long time after. She said, "That C.S. Fly, he should take all pictures of famous people in their underwear, and when they're not looking."

He found Bren Early where he should have looked first, the Chinaman's: Early sitting in the quiet room, though near the front this time, by one of the windows. He was sipping whiskey. On the table in front of him was a handwritten menu, in ink, and one of the Dana Moon "wanted" dodgers, Moon's face in the photo looking up at Bren Early.

Maurice Dumas left his cap and pulled up a chair. "The Chicago Kid," some of the others were calling him now. Or "Lucky Maurice." Luck, hell, it was sensing a story and digging for it, letting nothing discourage or deter. Go after it.

"Moon's wife didn't bring him the gun," Maurice said. He was going to add, flatly, "You did," but softened it at the last second. "I have a feeling it might have been you."

Bren Early was looking at the menu. He said, "Did you know this place is called The Oriental?"

"No, I didn't think it had a name."

"The Oriental," Early said.

Maurice waited a moment. "I also believe the company put up the five-thousand reward. Because I don't think the county would spend that kind of money on something that's — when you get right down to it — company business. Am I right or wrong?"

Early said, "Are you gonna have something to eat?"

"No, I don't think so."

"Well, if you aren't gonna eat, why don't you leave?"

Maurice felt a chill go up the back of his neck.

242

He managed to say, "I just thought we might talk."

"There's nothing to talk about," Early said.

"Well, maybe I will have something to eat, if it's all right."

Maurice ate some kind of pork dish, sitting there self-conscious, feeling he should have left and tried the man at a better time. Though Early did say one thing as he sipped his whiskey and then picked up the Moon "wanted" poster. He said, "A man who likes his front porch hasn't any business on one of these."

"No," Maurice said, to agree.

"Sometimes they put the wrong people on these things."

Early didn't say anything after that. He finished his whiskey and walked out, leaving the young reporter sitting there with his pork dish.

Chapter XII

1

Sundeen appeared in Sweetmary, picked up fresh mounts and supplies and went out again with twenty men, some eager new ones along. He'd hinted he was close to running Moon to ground, but would not give details. This time Maurice Dumas and several news reporters trailed after him, keeping well behind his dust.

There were saddle bums and gunnysackers who came up from around Charleston and Fairbank with Moon's "wanted" dodger folded in their pockets.

These men would study the pictures of Moon in Fly's gallery a long time, pretending to have keen looks in their eyes. They would drink whiskey in the saloons — all these ragtag chuck-line riders turned manhunters – talking in loud voices how they packed their .45-70's for distance or how an old Ballard could out-shoot a Henry. They would go out to their campsites along the Benson road, stare up at the Rincons and talk about dogging the man's sign clear to hell for that kind of reward money, come back here and buy a saloon with a whorehouse upstairs.

Best chance, everyone agreed, squat down in a blind and wait for the shot. Moon was bound to appear somewhere, though not likely to be snared and taken alive. Yes, it was up to chance; but some lucky bird would get the shot, come back with Moon wrapped in canvas and collect the $5,000; more money than could be made in ten years of herding and fence riding.

The saddle bums and gunnysackers straggled out in pairs and small groups, those who had soldiered saying they were going on an ex-tended campaign and would forage, live off the country. Most of them came dragging back in four or five days, hungry and thirsty, saying shit, Moon wasn't up there – like they had expected to find him sitting on a stump wait-ing. Wasn't anybody up there far as they could see.

How about Sundeen?

Him either.

The news reporters who had trailed out after
Sundeen came back with sore legs and behinds
– all of them except the Chicago Kid – to say
Phil Sundeen had not found anything either.
All he was doing was pushing his men up one
draw and down another, finding some empty
huts but not a sign of the mountain people.

Days went by. What seemed to be the last of
the manhunters came limping in with the same
story – nothing up there but wind and dry
washes – and looked around for old chums
who had gone out in other parties. A rough
tally indicated some had not returned. Were
they still hunting? Not likely, unless they were
living on mesquite beans. Were they dead? Or
had they gone home by way of Benson?

Ask Moon that one.

Ask him if you could ever find him. Or if he
was still up there. Maybe he had left here for
safer climes.

Like hell, said a man by the name of Asa
Bailey from Contention. He had seen Moon,
close enough to touch the tobacco wad in the
man's jaw.

The news reporters sat him down at a table
in the Gold Dollar with a full bottle, got out
their note pads and said, O.K., go ahead.

Asa Bailey told them there had been three of
them in the party and gave the names Wesley

246

and Urban as the other two — last seen headed southeast, having sworn off manhunting forever.

They had come across Sundeen and his bunch at the Moon place and Sundeen had run them off, telling them to keep their nose out of company business. They had stayed close enough to watch, though, and observed Sundeen riding off with most of his men, leaving two or three at the burnt-out house. Yes, Sundeen had set a torch to the place, though the roof and walls seemed in good shape.

Asa Bailey said he had been a contract guide out of Camp Grant some years before and knew Moon and his Apaches surely weren't going to stand around nor leave directions where they went. Moon would use his Apaches as his eyes and pull tricks to decoy Sundeen out of his boots: let him see a wisp of smoke up in the high reaches and Sundeen would take half a day getting up there to a cold fire set by some Apache woman or little kid. Let them wear themselves out and go home hungry, was Moon's game, all the time watching Sundeen.

"So we would play it too," Asa Bailey said, "pretend we was Moon and hang back off Sundeen's flank and sooner or later cross Moon's sign. Sundeen'd camp, we'd camp, rigging triplines, and making a circle around us with loose rocks we'd hear if somebody tried to approach.

"We were the stalkers, huh? Like hell. Imagine you're sitting all night in what you believe is an ambush. Dawn, you're asleep as Wesley and Urban are over a ways gathering the horses. You feel something — not hear it, *feel* it. And open your eyes in the cold gray light and not dare to even grunt. The man's hunched over you with the barrel tip of his six-gun sticking in your mouth. There he was with the kindly eyes and the tobacco wad you see in the pictures."

There wasn't a sound at that table until one of the newsmen said, "Well, what did he say?"

"What did he *say?* Nothing."

"Nothing at all?"

Asa Bailey reached across an angle of the table, grabbed the newsman by the shirtfront, drew his revolver and stuck it in the man's bug-eyed face, saying, "You want me to explain things to you or do you get the picture?"

2

Franklin Hovey, the company geologist, came in with a survey crew and two ore wagons of camp gear and equipment. Noticeably shaken, he said he would quit his job before going out with another survey party. "You don't *see* them," he said, "but there they are, like they rose out of the ground."

The news reporters finally got hold of him coming out of the telegraph office and practically bums-rushed him to the Gold Dollar. "Here, Franklin, something for your nerves." The reporters having a glass also since they were here.

"Whom did you telegraph?" they asked him.

"Mr. Vandozen. He must be apprised of what's happened."

The reporters raised their eyebrows and asked, "Well, what did happen out there?"

Franklin Hovey said his crew of eight had been working across a southwest section of the range at about seven thousand feet. One morning, three days ago, a tall nigger had appeared at their camp, came walking his horse in as they were sitting at the map table having breakfast. He gave them a polite good morning, said his name was Catlett and asked if they planned to blast hereabouts.

"I told him yes, and pointed to an outcropping of ledge along the south face that looked promising. I can't give you his exact words as the darkie said them, but he took off his old hat, scratched his wooly head and said, 'If you disturbs that rock, boss, it gwine come down in de canyon where de tanks at. Is you sure you wants to do that?' "

A couple of the reporters looked at each other with helpless expressions of pain, but no one interrupted the geologist. Franklin Hovey said, "See, there was a natural water tank in the canyon where they grazed a herd of horses. I told the darkie, 'That might be; but since the canyon is part of the company lease, we can blow it clear to hell if it strikes our fancy.' The darkie said something like, 'Strike yo fancy, huh?', not understanding the figure of speech. He said, 'Boss, we sees that rock come down in there, we-uns gwine strike yo fancy clean off this mountain.' I said, 'And who is the we-uns gwine do sech a thing as that?' "

Franklin sat back, beginning to relax with some liquor in him, glancing around the table to see if everyone appreciated his dialect. There were a couple of chuckles.

"The darkie himself smiled, knowing it was meant only as good-natured parody, and said, 'If y'all be so kind, jes don't mess the graze and the water. Awright, boss?'

"Now one of our powdermen went over to the wagon where we kept the explosives, got a stick of Number One and pointed it at the

250

darkie, saying — this was *not* good-natured, though I'll admit it was funny at the time. The powderman pointed the stick and said, 'How'd you like it if we tie this to your tail, Mr. Nig, with a lit fuse and see how fast it can send you home?' The darkie, Catlett, said, 'Yeah, boss, that would send a body home, I expects so.' He smiled again. But this time there was something different about his smile."

There was a silence. Those around the table could see by Franklin Hovey's expression he was thinking about that time again, that moment, as though realizing now it should have warned him, at least told him something.

"Did you blow the ledge?" a reporter asked.

"Yes, we did. Though we set off a small warning charge first to indicate our intention. I insisted we do that."

The reporters waited, seeing the next part coming, remembering the story Asa Bailey, the former contract guide, had told only a few days before.

"Our party was well armed," Franklin Hovey continued, "and we set a watch that night around the perimeter of the camp. As I've said, we were at about seven thousand feet on bare, open ground. With night guards on four sides and enough moonlight to see by, we were positive no one could sneak up to that camp."

251

"They hit you at dawn," a reporter said.

Others told him to shut up as Franklin Hovey shook his head.

"No, we arose, folded our cots, ate breakfast . . . dis*cussed* the darkie's threat while we were eating and, I remember, laughed about it, some of the others imitating him, saying, 'Yessuh, boss, ah's gwine strike yo fancy,' things like that. After breakfast we went over to the dynamite wagon to get what we'd need for the day — you might've seen it, a big ore wagon with a heavy canvas top to keep the explosives dry and out of the weather. One of the men opened the back end" — Franklin paused — "and they came out. They came out of the wagon that was in the middle of our camp, in the *middle*, our tents and the two other wagons surrounding it. They came *out* of it . . . the same colored man and another one and two Indians." Franklin shook his head, awed by the memory of it. "I don't even see how there was room in there with the fifty-pound cases, much less how they got in to begin with . . . Well, they held guns on us, took ours and threw them into the canyon . . . tied our hands in front of us and then tied the eight of us together in a line, arm to arm . . . while the one named Catlett took a dynamite cartridge, primed it with a Number Six detonator and crimped onto that about ten

252

feet of fuse, knowing exactly how to set the blasting cap in there and gather the end of the cartridge paper around it tight and bind it up good with twine. This man, I realized, knew how to shoot dynamite. I said, 'Now wait a minute, boy, we are only doing our job here, following orders.' The darkie said, 'Thas all ah'm doing too, boss. Gwine send y'all home.' I said to him again, 'Now wait a minute,' and the other members of the crew began to get edgy and speak up, saying we were only working men out here doing a job. The darkie said, 'Y'all doing a job awright, on our houses.' "

"Was Moon there?" a reporter asked.

"I told you," Franklin Hovey said, "it was the two colored men and two Apache Indians which, I forgot to mention, had streaks of yellowish-brown paint on their faces."

"The other colored man also began to prime sticks with blasting caps; so that between the two of them they soon had eight sticks of dynamite ready to fire, though not yet with the fuses attached. The one named Catlett approached me and poked a stick down into the front of my pants. Again, as you can imagine, I began to reason with him. He shook his head, pulled the stick out and walked around the line of us tied shoulder to shoulder and now placed the dynamite stick in my back pocket, saying,

'Yeah, tha's the place.'"

Many of the reporters were grinning and had to quickly put on a serious, interested expression as Franklin Hovey looked around the table.

"Well, they were behind us for several minutes, so we couldn't see what they were doing. Then they placed a stick of Number One, which will shatter solid rock into small fragments — they placed a stick in every man's back pocket or down into his pants if he didn't have a pocket. Then came around in front of us again and began drawing the fuses out between our legs, laying each one on the ground in about a ten-foot length.

"I forgot to mention they had found a box of cigars in somebody's gear and all four of them were puffing away on big stogies, blowing out the smoke as they stood about with their weapons, watching us. But not laughing or carrying on, as you might expect. No, they appeared serious and very calm in their manner.

"The tall colored man, Catlett, said something and the four of them began lighting the ends of the fuses with their cigars.

"Well, we began to pull and push against each other. We tried to reason — or maybe I should say plead with them by this time — seeing those fuses burning at eighteen seconds a foot, which seems slow, huh? Well, I'll tell you, those sputtering, smoking fuse ends were racing, not crawling, right there coming toward our legs. 'Stomp 'em out!' somebody yelled and all of us began dancing and stomping the ground before the burning ends were even close. The two colored men and the Apaches had moved back a ways. Now they raised their rifles, pointed 'em right at us and Catlett said, 'Stand still. You move, we'll shoot you dead.' "

Franklin Hovey waited, letting his listeners think about it.

"Which would you prefer, to be shot or blown up?" he said. "If you chose the former, I'd probably agree. But you would *not* choose it, I guarantee, looking into the muzzles of their guns. I promise you you'd let that fuse burn through between your feet at its pace and by then try not to move a muscle while being overcome by pure fear and terrible anguish. There was a feeling of us pressing against each other, rooted there, but not one of us stomped on a fuse. It burned between our feet and was out of sight behind us, though we could hear it and smell the powder and yarn burning. With maybe a half minute left to live, I closed my eyes. I waited. I waited some more. There was an awful silence."

And silence at the table in the Gold Dollar.

"I could not hear the fuse burning. Nothing. I opened my eyes. The four with the guns stood watching us, motionless. It was like the moment had passed and we knew it, but still not one of us moved."

Franklin Hovey let the reporters and listeners around the table wait while he finished the whiskey in his glass and passed the back of his hand over his mouth.

"The fuses," he said then, "had not been connected to the dynamite sticks, but burned to the ends a few feet behind us. It was a warning, to give us a glimpse of eternity. The tall one, Catlett, approached and said if they ever saw us again, well, we'd just better not come back. They hitched a team to the dynamite wagon and drove off with close to a thousand pounds of high explosives."

"That's it, huh?" a reporter said. "What was it the nigger said to you?"

"I told you, he gave us a warning."

"Just said, don't come back?"

Franklin Hovey seemed about to explain, elaborate, then noticed that two of the girls who worked in the Gold Dollar were in the crowd of listeners.

"He said something, well, that wasn't very nice."

"We see you again, we crimp the fuse on,

stick the dynamite stick up your ass and shoot you to the moon . . . boy," were Bo Catlett's exact words.

3

A man by the name of Gean was brought down in a two-wheel Mexican cart lying cramped in the box with his new straw hat on his chest, both legs shattered below the knees by a single .50-caliber bullet. He said he felt it, like a scythe had swiped off his legs, before he even heard the report; that's how far away the shooter was. He said he should never have left the railroad. If he ever went back he would be some yard bull, hobbling after tramps on his crutches, if the company doctor was able to save his legs.

The one who had guided the cart down out of the mountains was Maurice Dumas. The Chicago Kid was tired, dirty and irritable and did not say much that first day. He took Gean to the infirmary where there were all manner of crushed bones from mine and mill accidents, some healing, some turning black, lying there in a row of cots. It smelled terrible in the infirmary and the reporters who came to interview Gean handed him a bottle and asked only a few questions.

Had Sundeen found Moon?

Shit, no. It was the other way around.

Moon was carrying the fight now?

Teasing, pecking at Sundeen's flanks.

Was it Moon who shot him?

Get busted from five hundred yards, who's to say? But it's what he would tell his grandchildren. Yes, I was shot by Dana Moon himself back in the summer of '93 and lived to tell about it. Maybe.

How many men did Moon have?

A ghost band. Try and count them.

What about the Mexicans?

They'd come across women and children, ask them, Where they at? No savvy, mister. We'd burn the crops and move on.

And the colored?

The niggers? Same thing. Few Indin women and little wooly-headed breeds. Where's your old man at? Him gone. Him gone where? Me no know, be home by-'m-by. Shit, let's go. But it was at a nigger place the sniping had begun . . . riding off from the house after loading up with chuck and leading a steer . . . ba-*wang*, this rifle shot rang out, coming from, I believe, California, and we broke for cover. When we looked back, there was one of ours laying in the

258

weeds. After it happened two times Sundeen had a fit, men getting picked off and all you could see up in the rocks was puffs of smoke. But he took care of that situation.

How did he do that?

Well, he took hostages so they wouldn't fire at us. I was walking up a grade toward a line shack, smoke wisping out the chimney, I got cut down and lay there looking at sky till one of your people found me and saved my life. Though I won't pay him a dime for that bed-wagon ride back here; I been sick ever since.

What else—how about Indians?

Shit, the only Indians he'd ever seen in his life was fort Indins and diggers. The ones rode for Moon were slick articles or wore invisible warpaint, for they had not laid eyes on a one.

The company doctor took off Gean's right leg. Gean said he could have done it back home under an El Paso & Southwestern freight car and saved the fare from New Mexico.

4

My, that Gean has the stuff, doesn't he? Tough old bird.

Maurice Dumas said to Bill Wells of the *St.*

Louis Globe-Democrat, "Everybody was so taken with his spunk, or anxious to get out of there, they didn't ask the right question."

"About what?"

"The hostages. He said they took hostages, then started talking about how I found him and put him in the cart."

"What about the hostages?"

"They shot them," Maurice said.

He wasn't sure he was going to tell this until he did, sitting with Bill Wells in the New Alliance. Like one reporter confiding in another. What should I do? Should I reveal what happened or not?

Why not?, was the question, Bill Wells said. "Are you afraid of Sundeen?"

"Of course I am," Maurice said.

"We have power, all of us together, that even the company wouldn't dare to buck," Bill Wells said. It was a fact, though at the moment Bill Wells was glad they had come to this miners' saloon rather than mix with the crowd at the Gold Dollar. "Tell me what happened."

Maybe Sundeen thought it would be an easy trip: march up there with his hooligans and run the people off their land, burn their homes and crops, scatter the herds — like Sherman marching to the sea. Sundeen did have an air

260

about him at first, as though he knew what he was doing.

But there were not that many mountain people to run off. And how did you burn adobe except to blacken it up some? Tear down a house, the people would straggle back and build another. The thing Sundeen had to do was track down the leaders and deal with them face to face.

But how did you find people who did not leave a trail? Even the cold camps they did find were there to misdirect and throw them off the track. Sundeen's men began to spit and growl and Sundeen himself became more abusive in his speech, less confident in his air.

They had burned a field of new corn when one of Sundeen's tail-end riders was shot out of his saddle. The next day it happened again. One rifle shot, one dead.

Sundeen came to a Mexican goat farm early in the morning, tore through the house and barn, flushed assorted women and kids, ah!, and three grown men that brought a squinty light to Sundeen's eyes. He tried to question them in his Sonora-whorehouse Spanish — no doubt missing his old segundo — and even hit them some with leather gloves on, drawing blood. Where's Moon? No answer. *Smack*, he'd throw a fist into that impassive dark face and the man would be knocked to the ground. The women and children cried and carried on, but the three men never said a word. Sundeen tied their hands behind them and loaded them into that two-wheeled cart with a mule to pull it and had them lead his column when he moved on.

But then, you see, he didn't draw any sniper fire and that seemed to aggravate him more than having his men picked off.

Soon after taking the hostages they woke up in the morning to find half their horses gone, disappeared from the picket rope. Sundeen sent riders to Sweetmary for a new string. They came back to report the story of the survey crew being hit.

It was in a high meadow facing a timbered slope and a little shack perched up in the rocks above that Sundeen, all of a sudden, reached the end of his skimpy patience. It was no doubt seeing the smoke coming out of the stovepipe. Somebody was up there, a quarter of a mile away. And he was sure they were in the timber also, in the deep pine shadows. There was not a sound when he began to yell.

"Moon! Come on out! . . . You and your boogers, Moon! . . . Let's get it done!"

His words echoed out there and faded to nothing.

Sundeen pulled the three Mexicans from the cart and told them to move out in the meadow, keep going, then yelled for them to stop when they were about forty yards off. They stood in the sun bareheaded, looking up at the timber and turning to look back at Sundeen who brought all his riders up along the edge of the meadow, spread out in a line.

He yelled now, "You see it, Moon? . . . Show yourself or we'll blow out their lights!"

Nothing moved in the pines. The only sound, a low moan of wind coming off the escarpment above.

The three men, bareheaded and in white, hands tied behind them, didn't know which way to face, to look at the silent trees or at the rifles pointed at them now.

"I've given him enough warning," Sundeen said. "He's heard it, isn't that right? If he's got ears he heard it." If he's up there, somebody said. "He's up there, I know he is," Sundeen said. "Man's been watching us ten days, scared to come out. All right, I give him a chance, haven't I?" He looked up and yelled out once more, "Moon?" Waited a moment and said, "Shit . . . go ahead, fire."

"And they killed them?"
Maurice nodded.

"But if he knew you were a witness —"

"He'd forgotten I was along by then, other things on his mind."

Bill Wells was thoughtful, then asked, "Was Moon up there, in the trees?"

"Somebody was. Shots were fired and Sundeen divided his men to come at the timber from two sides. That was when Gean was shot."

"And you were considering you might keep it a secret?"

"I wasn't sure how I felt. I mean I've never handled anything like this before," Maurice said. "Though I know we're sworn to print the truth, letting the chips fall where they may."

"Or stack the chips against the company's hand," Bill Wells said, the idea bringing a smile. "Yes, I can see Vandozen squirming and sweating now."

Chapter XIII

1

There was a framed slate in the Gold Dollar, back of the bar, that gave the betting odds on a Sundeen-Moon showdown:

2 – 1 one week
5 – 1 four days
10 – 1 two days

It meant you could bet one dollar to win two if you thought Sundeen would track down Moon and bring him in dead or alive within one week. The house was betting against it ever happening. When a week passed and Sundeen hadn't returned, you lost your dollar. For shorter periods you could bet the higher odds that were posted.

265

When Sundeen returned a few days ago with four men face-down over their saddles and the rest of his troop worn raw and ugly, they erased the old odds and wrote on the slate:

4 – 1 one week
10 – 1 four days
20 – 1 two days
100 – 1 one day

A miner at the bar, who had not seen the new odds before, said, "I'd hide that thing was I you. Case he comes in here."

"Who, Mr. Sundeen?" said Ed O'Day, who ran the Gold Dollar and sometimes served behind the bar. "He wants to bet on himself we'd be glad to cover it. Or, he wants to bet against himself I'm sure there some takers. Making a wager isn't anything personal. The man is not gonna bet against himself and take a dive, is he? No, not in this kinda contest. So, he thinks he's gonna come out the victor, let him put up his money."

Ed O'Day was a known high-roller; he ran faro, monte and poker tables in the back of his place and would bet either side of an issue depending on the odds.

Bren Early stepped toward them, moving his

elbow along the polished edge of the bar. He said, "You're betting against him finding Moon is all you're doing."

"Mr. Early, how are you? Sorry I didn't see you there. The usual?"

Bren nodded. The slight — not being noticed immediately — was as much an insult to him as the odds board: putting Sundeen against Moon and ignoring him completely. Bren had a hard knot inside his stomach. He wanted to cut this barkeeper down, level him with a quiet remark that had an eternal ring. (Something to do with, serving these miners and tourists, "What would you know about putting your life on the line?" Or, ". . . What would you know about facing death?") But he couldn't think of the words when he was on edge like this. Goddamn it.

Pouring him a whiskey, Ed O'Day said, "Finding Moon is ninety percent of it, yes. If that ever happens it would be a different story."

"How would you set the odds then?" Bren asked, satisfied that his tone did not show the edge.

"Well, I'm inclined to believe they would favor Mr. Sundeen. I don't mean as a shooting contest. I mean if he runs him down the game's over."

"How do you come to that?" Bren asked the know-it-all, feeling the knot tighten.

Ed O'Day looked both ways along the bar and leaned closer as he said, "You take a person raised on sour milk and make him look dumb in front of his fellow man — You see what I mean? He ever sets eyes on Moon he's gonna kill him."

"You know that as fact," Bren said.

"No, but I'd bet on it."

"You heard right now Sundeen had located him — you'd put your money on Sundeen?"

"I'd say it would be the safer bet."

"Turn the same odds around?"

Ed O'Day hesitated. "You said if he locates him —"

"Gets Moon to stand still and fight."

"Just Sundeen, or his men too?"

"His men, anybody he wants to bring along."

The miner standing next to Bren said, "Anybody or everybody? The way he's signing up people, he's gonna be taking a army next time — saying up at the works the next time's the last time. Though I don't want to mess up your bet none."

"That's talk," Ed O'Day said, but looked at Bren Early to get his reaction.

"No, it's fact," the miner said. "Sundeen sent to Bensons, St. David, Fairbank — twenty a week, grub and quarters. Most the miners want to quit and join up; but Selkirk told him no, he couldn't hire no miners. See, he's gonna take all the men he can find and not come back till it's done."

The miner's heavy mustache, showing fine traces of gray, reminded Bren of Moon. He wondered what Moon was doing this minute. Squinting at heat waves for signs of dust. Or tending his guns, wiping down Old Certain Death with an oil rag. Damn.

"I don't care how many people he raises," Bren said, "I want to know what odds you're giving if both sides stand to shoot and you want Sundeen . . . ten to one?"

"*Ten* to one?" Ed O'Day said. "Talking about if the two sides ever meet."

"No bet less they do."

"Doesn't matter how many men Sundeen has?"

"He can hire the U.S. Army," Bren said.

"Ten to one," Ed O'Day said and thought about it some more. "Well, it's interesting if we're talking about real money."

"Give me a Maricopa bank check," Bren said.

Ed O'Day went over to the cash register and came back with the check, an ink pot and a pen.

Bren leaned over the bar and scratched away

for a minute, picked up the check to blow on it, wave it in the air, and laid it on the polished surface again.

"Seven thousand Sundeen goes out and never comes back."

Ed O'Day, who wore the same expression drawing a pair of aces he did picking his teeth, said, "Is this the bet we been talking about all along?"

"I'm cutting out the only-if's and what-if's," Bren said. "Sundeen comes back for any reason after he leaves — if it's just to go to the toilet, this check is yours. But when he doesn't, and you learn he's dead, you pay off ten to one. Which is what?"

"Comes to seventy thousand," Ed O'Day answered, like it was no more than a day's take.

"This man here is our witness," Bren said. "Have him write his name on the check somewhere."

The miner looked from Bren to Ed O'Day with his mouth partly open. "You're paying him seventy thousand dollars if Sundeen gets killed?"

"No different'n writing life insurance," Ed O'Day said and winked at Bren —

Who felt good now and didn't mind at all the man's cocksure coyness.

"I'll even pay double if he gets struck by

270

lightning," Ed O'Day said.

Bren let an easy grin form, as if in appreciation, though there was more grin inside him than out.

He said, "You never can tell."

2

"All the people," a reporter sitting on the Congress front porch said. You would think the circus was in town. It is, another reporter said; featuring Phil Sundeen and his wild animal show. Christ, look at them. Bunch of range bums and bushwackers trying to pass as Quantrill's guerrillas.

Bren found Maurice Dumas sitting in the lobby staring at nothing. When he asked what was the matter, Maurice said he was thinking of going home; watching innocent people get shot was not his idea of covering a war. Bren said, no, when men fought without honor it was a sorry business.

"But we're gonna teach them a lesson, partner, and I sure hope you're here to see it."

Maurice perked up. "You're getting into it?"

Bren nodded.

"When?"

"I'll tell you," Bren said, "this looks like it's gonna be my busy night. If you could help me out some I guarantee you'll be in the front row when the fireworks go off."

"Get what things done?"

"Find Sundeen first. Tell him I'll meet him at the Chinaman's, the Oriental in about an hour."

"You mean —"

"Unh-unh," Bren said, "that's what I don't want to happen by mistake, ahead of time. Tell him I got something important to say. No guns. You'll inspect him and he can have somebody inspect me if he wants. Tell him it's the answer to how to end this deal and that he's gonna like it."

"I don't know if I can stand to speak to him." Maurice said.

"Listen, you write this story they'll make you the editor. Don't let personal feelings get in your way. The other thing —" Bren paused, looking around the lobby. He said, "Come on," and led Maurice to the back hall where the first-floor rooms were located. The light from the wall fixtures was dim, but it was quiet here, private. Bren took a thick envelope from his pocket and handed it to Maurice.

"List of some things I'm gonna need and the money to buy 'em with. Open it."

Maurice did.

"Put the money in your pocket."

"Looks like a lot."

"Two hundred dollars is all."

Maurice unfolded a sheet of paper. It was Moon's "wanted" dodger.

"You'll see the notes on there I've written."

"Yeah?" Maurice read them, then gave Bren a funny look, frowning. "You serious? You want this printed?"

"Trust me and don't ask questions, it's part of the scheme," Bren said. "You'll see where to get everything; it's all on the list. The case of whiskey, buy something good. The pack animal and cross-buck, I wouldn't pay more than fifty dollars. What else? It's going on seven o'clock, how about we meet at the livery stable eleven thirty, quarter of twelve. Sound good?"

"I don't know if I can have everything by then." Maurice looked worried now.

But not Bren. He said, "Hey, are you kidding me? Anybody rises as early as you is a natural-born go-getter."

Vandozen, seated in the middle of the settee, seemed to blend with the room, belong: formal but relaxed in his light-gray business suit and wing collar; pinch-nose glasses hanging from a black ribbon, resting on his vest.

Janet Pierson said, "Mr. Vandozen is here." Saying it as Bren came through the kitchen and the two men were already face to face. "He's been waiting for you. I asked him if he'd like some coffee —"

"How about cognac?" Bren said.

Vandozen nodded. "A small one. Mrs. Pierson was kind enough to let me wait."

"I didn't know you were in town." Bren glanced at Janet.

Vandozen watched her go out to the kitchen as he said, "I built a place near Lordsburg, to be close to our New Mexico operations, some good ones just getting started." His gaze returned to Bren who was seated now in an easy chair, his hat off, coat open. "I can be here overnight on the Southern Pacific, but I hadn't planned on coming as often as I have."

"No, this kind of business," Bren said, "you don't plan its twists and turns, do you?"

"We're going to end it," Vandozen said. "I

want you to go out, talk to this Moon. Tell him we'll make a deal with him."

"What kind of deal?" Bren said, taken by surprise. Jesus Christ, he didn't want any *deal*. Not now. He stared at Vandozen sitting on that velvet settee like it was his throne.

"You're going to arrange a meeting between this Moon and myself." Vandozen paused, his gaze moving as Janet came in with a decanter and two brandy snifters, and watched her as she served them, saying, "Very nice. Thank you."

Bren remained silent, edgy now. Damn. Seeing his plan coming apart. He said, "It's dark in here. Why don't you turn up the lamps?"

"It's fine," Vandozen said. "Though you can close that front window if you don't mind."

There were occasional sounds from outside, men's voices in the street: first-shift miners returning to their quarters, some of them a little drunk.

Jesus Christ, whose house was it? Bren said, "What do you want to talk for? Your man's going out again; he'll get it done."

"He's *not* getting it done," Vandozen said, with emphasis but more quietly than Bren had spoken. "This business should have been handled quickly with a show of force. Offer one choice, leave, that's all. What does he do, stumbles around, can't even find them. When he does, he ties up three Mexicans and shoots them with a newspaperman as a witness. Which is going to take some countering, not to mention money."

"It's gonna be over soon," Bren said.

"I know it is. You bring this Moon to me and and we'll make a deal."

"His name's Dana . . . Dana Moon," Bren said.

"That's fine. Go get him. Tell him we'll meet at his office or mine, I don't care. Criminal charges against him will be dropped. We'll pay for – no, we'll work out some plan of assistance for anyone whose home or crops were damaged. Tell him any future survey work will be done in isolated areas."

Bren said, "Ah, now we're getting to it. You haven't found the copper you thought you would, huh?"

"I can say test samples have been misleading, promising more than the locations would ever yield," Vandozen said. "But that's beside the point. I made an error in judgment, this business going on; allowed it to take on far more prominence – considerably more of my time than it's worth. So you and I are going to bring it to a halt."

"I don't believe it's part of my job," Bren

said, "since I'm not a messenger boy."

Vandozen looked at him for what seemed a long time, though perhaps only ten seconds. "What *is* your job?" he asked.

"I don't know. Tell me."

"Isn't this Moon a friend of yours?"

"*Dana* Moon."

"You two, I understand, used to be close friends?"

"What's that got to do with it?"

"Don't you want to help him?"

"Dana can handle it himself."

"For God's sake —" Janet Pierson said.

The two men looked at her seated in the straight chair, away from them.

"I'm sorry," she said. "I didn't mean to interrupt."

"Mrs. Pierson understands," Vandozen said. "Or, I should say, she doesn't understand why you don't want to help our friend." Still with the quiet tone.

"I didn't say I wouldn't help him."

"Or why you don't want to help the company. You're a stockholder . . . making, what?, ten thousand dollars a year. Why would you knowingly act in violation of your contract?"

"Knowing what?"

"Well, doing anything that's not in the company's best interest. That's standard in any

277

employee contract."

"The fine print, huh?"

"You don't recall reading that?"

Bren didn't answer. He sat with his cognac, looking at Vandozen, a question in his mind, but afraid Vandozen's answer would destroy his plan completely. Still he had to ask it.

"What about Sundeen?" You call him off?"

"Not yet."

Bren let his breath out slowly. "When you gonna see him?"

"He's to see me first thing in the morning."

"So he doesn't know about this yet."

"He'll be fired five minutes after he walks in the office."

Bren sat in the deep chair another moment, comfortable, beginning to feel pretty good, yes, confident again. He finished his cognac and pulled himself out of the chair.

"Well, I might as well get going. You'll know something tomorrow."

Janet Pierson said, "Do you mind? It's stuffy in here."

Vandozen watched her raise the window and stand looking out, her back to him.

"Why does he have to go tonight?"

"Because he's childish," Vandozen said. "He has to go out and kick rocks, or run his horse

278

till it lathers." He reached over to place his glass on the end table and sat back again.

"He is like a little boy," Janet said.

"Yes, he is . . . Why don't you come over here?" Vandozen watched her turn from the window. "Come on . . . sit here."

When she was next to him, on the edge of the settee, he put his hand on her shoulder and brought her gently back against the cushion. His hand remained as he said, "Tell him you're leaving."

She looked at his face that was lined but not weathered, the skin on his neck loose, crepe-like, in the starched white collar.

"I admired you when you admitted you'd make a mistake."

"Not a mistake, a misjudgment. Come to Lordsburg with me."

"Don't you have a wife?"

"In New Jersey. Not in New Mexico, Colorado or Arizona."

"I admired the way you never raised your voice, even when you said things with feeling."

"Yes," Vandozen said, drawing her against his shoulder, "in certain areas I have firm convictions and feelings."

4

Bren sat at a corner table in the Oriental. He let Sundeen take his time and look around. When Sundeen finally came over he pulled out the chair across from Bren and sat down.

"Now then," Sundeen said, "where were we?"

"They're trying to call the game." Bren sat with his hands flat on the table. "Vandozen says he's had enough of your monkeyshines. He's gonna fire you tomorrow, and all those hoboes you got riding for you."

Sundeen nodded, not surprised. "You would think he had something personal to do with this." He sat back in his Douglas chair saying, "Shit."

"There's hope," Bren said, "if you can get your misfits out of town before morning. He can't find you, he can't fire you, can he?"

"I don't know — don't many of 'em snap to as they should," Sundeen said. "There's some mean Turks, but most of 'em ain't worth cow shit."

"How many you need? . . . How many does Moon have?"

"Who in the hell knows? All I seen was women and little kids."

280

"Some Mexicans with their hands tied, I understand."

"And their eyes open. They knew what they were doing. I cut the ropes, let 'em hold their old cap-n-balls, they'd still be dead, wouldn't they? I lost men blown to hell from a distance. Are we talking about rules of some kind or what?"

"We're getting off the track," Bren said.

"You're the one called this," Sundeen said, his snarly, ugly nature peeking through. "We can settle up right now, you want, and quit talking about it."

"You got spirit," Bren said, "but save it and let's do this show with a little style. You don't want to meet in some back alley; you got a reputation to think of — as poor as it is."

"Jesus," Sundeen said, on the edge now, hands gripping the arms of his chair.

Like working a wild stallion, hold him on the line, but don't let him break his neck. Bren said, "If you're big enough to handle your men, gather 'em and head up to White Tanks. I'll get Moon, whatever people he's got . . . You come up the draw and we'll meet at his place."

Sundeen said, "Through that steep-sided chute? You must believe I'm dumb."

"Scout it. Turn all the rocks over, you want. I'm talking about we meet at the top, have a

281

stand-up battle like we had in Sonora. Quit this tracking around and do the thing right." Bren paused. Sundeen remained silent. "Unless you lack the gristle."

Sundeen said, "You don't need to prod, if that's what you're doing. I'm thinking." And said then, "Why don't we meet at White Tanks?"

"Moon won't do it, I'll tell you that right now. He'll fight for his home, but not for any government layout. He doesn't look at this the way you and I do."

Sundeen was thoughtful again. "It would make some noise, wouldn't it?"

"Hear it clear across the country," Bren said. "Get your name in the history book."

Sundeen grinned then, tickled. "Jesus Christ, is this the way it's done?"

"Why not? Better than maybe we meet sometime maybe we don't."

"Well . . . Moon's place then. I guess it's as good as another."

As Sundeen got up, Bren said, "Whatever happened to that old segundo of yours?"

"Ruben Vega," Sundeen said. "He tried to change sides and didn't make it."

"That's too bad. He seemed a good one for his age."

"Yeah, he was quicker than most," Sundeen

said, "but in this game there ain't any second prize, is there?"

5

The sound jolted Bruckner awake: something dropped on his desk. Somebody standing there.

Maurice said, "The printer over at the paper asked me to give these to you."

"What?" Bruckner said. "The hell you want?"

Maurice stepped back from the man's stale whiskey odor. "You're supposed to post them around right away. Printer said it was ordered from the county."

Bruckner rubbed a hand over his face, opened his eyes and the squirt reporter was gone. He looked at his watch: twenty past twelve; heard horses outside and turned to his window.

Three horses out there . . . the squirt news reporter mounting and another fella already up, leading a packhorse with gear and a wood crate lashed to the cross-buck. Bruckner watched them head down LaSalle Street into darkness.

When he turned to his desk again he frowned and said out loud, "What in the hell —" Bren

Early's photo was looking at him from a stack
of "wanted" dodgers that said:

$5,000
REWARD

(Dead or Alive)

for information leading to
the arrest or seizure of

CAPT. BRENDAN EARLY

wanted for the killing of
P. Sundeen (and probably others)
Approach with utmost caution!!!

Chapter XIV

1

Kate said to Moon, "What do you need all those enemies for when you got a friend like Bren Early?"

Moon said, "How long you want to live in a line-camp and cook outside in the weather? It's a way to get it done and move back in our home."

"If you win," she said.

Moon said, "I don't worry about that part till I'm there."

"Do you think it makes sense?"

Moon had taken his wife aside for this chat, away from the others sitting around the tents and brush wickiups of the camp, one of the high-up Apache rancherías.

He said to Kate, "Don't look at it as a

sensible person would. Try to see it through Bren's eyes first, the chance to do battle and win some medals."

"Who gives him the medals?"

"You know what I mean — add to his stature. He missed the war and he's been moaning about it ever since. Now he sees a chance to win fame and get his picture in the paper, big."

"At whose expense?" Kate said.

"You got to look at it another way too," Moon said. "Sundeen is gonna dog us till we put an end to him. I'd rather meet him across the wall than keep looking over my shoulder . . . worrying about you at home the times I'm gone."

"Now you make it sound like a just cause," Kate said, "but I believe the idea tickles you as much as Bren."

"No, not that much," Moon said, feeling itchy, excited, but trying not to show it. "Come on."

They walked back through the pines to the ranchería, past the children and the squat Mimbre women at the cookfires, to where Bren was sitting on his bedroll, Maurice Dumas next to him. The Apaches had sighted them early this morning and brought them up to the camp. The case of whiskey had been opened and a bottle passed around as they discussed this business of meeting Sundeen. The whiskey

and learned that Nathan Bedford
facing him with a force of 7,000.
what Sooy did?

Moon said, interested.

—" Kate said.

ce Dumas watched and listened, fasci-

er in the morning the mountain people
an to arrive at the stone house with the
rred furniture in the yard:

Bo Catlett, Thomas Jefferson and two more
n "US" braces and worn cavalry boots. Bo said
they had flipped coins and the ones lost had to
stay home with the families and the herds.
They had a talk with Moon and Bren Early, got
Bren to agree to an idea and the 10th Cavalry
veterans went down into the barranca with two
fifty-pound cases of dynamite.

Young Eladio Duro, Alfonso with his
cartridge belts, and six farmers carrying old
Ballards and Remingtons represented their families. (Others were scattered and could not be
notified.) Eladio wore a green sash, a sword and
a caplock Dragoon pistol his grandfather had
carried at Resaca de la Palma. Everyone full of
war.

Red and his seven Mimbres squatted in the
yard with a clay pot of ochre paint; with bowls

was good after nearly a month of sour cornbeer.
The talk was good. The idea seemed good, too.
But did it make sense? Or didn't it have it?

Bo Catlett was here and another former 10th
cavalryman by the name of Thomas Jefferson.
Eladio Duro, the son of Armando, was here
with a heavily armed farmer named Alfonso
who wore three belts of bullets. Red was here
— it was his camp — with seven Mimbre
Apache males who remained silent and let Red
speak for them — as he was doing now in
halting Spanish.

When he finished Bo Catlett said, "It seem
that way," and looked at Bren Early. "Captain,
Red say, do these people want to die? Or is it us
want to die?"

"Tell him," Bren said, "these people will
never stop hunting him as long as they live, or
we let them live."

"He knows all about that," Bo Catlett said.
"He wants to know, what is this standing and
waiting for your enemy to come at you?"

"Tell him it's the way white men face each
other with honor. I mean civilized people,"
Bren said to Bo. "It's the way we've always done
it."

"Tell him *that*?" Bo Catlett said, glancing at
Moon and back to Bren. "You gonna have to
explain it to *me* first. Lest you plan to bush-

wack him in the draw. We got seven hundred pounds of dynamite could help."

"Artillery," Bren said, and was thoughtful a moment. "I told him he could bring his men up. Gave him my word on that."

Bo Catlett translated into Spanish and Moon watched Red and his Mimbres as they looked at one another.

"They think you must be drunk," Moon said to Bren. "Let me make a speech for a minute."

He spoke in Spanish, for the benefit of the Apaches and the Mexican farmers, though Bo Catlett's people were included. Moon said that some of this business with Sundeen was personal and he didn't expect anyone to fight because of something that happened a long time ago in Sonora. But Sundeen and his people also represented the company and the company wanted this land.

"Tell them it's a question of honor," Bren said. "Oh-*nohr*."

"It's a question of how you want to live," Moon said in Spanish. "My business isn't to hide and shoot at them the rest of my life. I have other things I want to do." He looked at Kate. "But I can't do them until I finish this. Can we win? I believe so. I believe the company will look at us and decide it isn't worth all the time and money and they'll go somewhere

288

else for their copper." M⸻ Bren. "In fact, I'm ⸻ hasn't sent somebo⸻

Bren didn't m⸻ to think of somet⸻

"— but I believe th⸻ see we're determined t⸻

"That's it," Bren said. "⸻ final show of strength. And ⸻ fail, they'll cave in."

Moon seemed to accept this. ⸻ some of us die?" And looked at ⸻ Alfonso. "Some of us already have. But ⸻ rather face them now than risk being sh⸻ the back planting corn. Maybe you don't like ⸻ fight this way. I don't blame you. But this is ⸻ the way it is."

When Moon appeared finished, Bren said, "Did you mention honor? It didn't sound very inspiring."

Moon said, "It's their lives. It's up to them."

Following the trail down from the ranchería, Moon close to Kate, he wanted to talk to her, be near her. But Bren rode a length behind and told how Sooy Smith had entered Okolona and captured a big bunch of Rebel officers and men on furlough, February 17, 1864 — Bren full of war again — February 20, 3:00 P.M. reached a point south of Prairie Station with

289

two brigades ⸻
Forrest was ⸻
You know ⸻
"What?" ⸻
"God ⸻
Mauri⸻
nated.⸻
La⸻
beg⸻
ch⸻

of *atole*, the flour gruel they would eat as their last meal before battle; with small leather sacks of *hoddentin*, the magic powder that would protect them from bullets; with cigars and tulapai, the corn-beer, and chants that reminded them they were the *Shis-Inday*, the invincible Apache . . . the chosen ones. Those not chosen for this — another twenty in Red's band — were in the thicket behind the house, up on the escarpment and watching the back trails. (Sundeen would have to come straight at them up the barranca, and not pull any sneaky tricks.)

Bren unloaded and reloaded his .44 Russians and his fancy Merwin & Hulberts and shoved a seven-cartridge tube into the stock of his polished Spencer . . . ready for war, brimming over with it, telling Moon how Sooy Smith had dug in to make a stand at Ivey's Farm against Barteau who had taken over for Tyree Bell, see, when Tyree Bell had become sick . . . confusing but, to Moon, a good sound; it matched the excitement he felt.

Maurice Dumas spent some time inside the smoke-blackened house with Kate, helping her as she baked about a dozen loaves of bread, but most of the time looking out the window at the Apaches and the Mexican farmers, at Moon and Early out by the adobe wall.

291

It was exciting and it was scary, too. Maurice wondered if he was the only one who felt it. Everyone else seemed so calm, or resigned. He said to Kate, "The thing is, they don't *have* to do this."

"Yes, they do," Kate said. "They believe they do, which is the same thing."

"Twenty-two," Maurice said, "against however many Sundeen brings. Probably twice as many."

"Twenty-three," Kate said, finished with the bread, loading a Henry now with .44's.

"*You're* gonna take part in this?"

"It's my house too," Kate said.

In a little while Moon sent Maurice Dumas down to White Tanks to tell Sundeen he could come any time he wanted.

2

Someone had brought the Capt. Brendan Early dodger, ". . . wanted for the killing of P. Sundeen," and showed it around. Sundeen read it and shook his head, pretending to be amused, but did not think it was funny. The news reporters at White Tanks quoted him as saying, "I hope there is money on that son of a

– –'s head, for I am sure as – – going to collect it."

Yes, the news reporters had finally come to the field, brought by the message Maurice Dumas had left displayed in the hotel lobby: *Come to White Tanks for final showdown, Rincon Mountains War. Scheduled to begin around noon today!* Bren Early's idea. ("Why do you want all them?" Maurice had asked him. Bren's answer: "The more people there are who sympathize with our fight against the giant company, the more likely the company is to back off." Now it was *our* fight.)

When Maurice came down the mountain to White Tanks and saw the crowd, he couldn't believe it. Riders, wagons, buggies, Indians, a few women, little kids playing on the fence around the stock pen – there must have been two hundred people or more. When he reached the agency buildings and began sorting everybody out, Maurice found that maybe half were spectators, gawkers, and the rest were in the pay of Sundeen . . . something like a hundred armed men!

Had Bren Early counted on that many opposing them? Not by half, Maurice recalled. Perhaps forty men at the most.

But one *hundred* – all hard-eyed cutthroats in a variety of getups: derbies, straws, sombreros, dusty business suits and batwing chaps . . . shotguns, rifles, six-shooters, all were armed with at least two guns; they stood about talking, drinking whiskey, checking and fooling with their weapons . . . talking in loud, confident voices and finding, it seemed, a great deal to laugh about.

My God.

C.S. Fly was not present. Maurice learned the famed photographer had declined the invitation, saying he had pictures enough for a fools' gallery as is. However there were others — among them A. Frank Randall of Willcox and someone representing Beuhman & Hartwell of Tucson — busy taking pictures of Sundeen, groups of his cutthroats holding rifles and revolvers, and some of the White Tanks reservation Indians who posed, not having any idea what was going on.

Maurice had to push through a crowd on the porch of the agency office to get to Sundeen inside, sitting with his boots propped up on Moon's desk and telling the news reporters his riders would "bite shallow" else they would eat those people up in two minutes. Maurice waited for Sundeen to notice him, then said, "They're ready for you."

Sundeen eyed him. "How many people's he got?"

"I'm not at liberty to say."

"At *liberty*," Sundeen said, drawing up out of the swivel chair. "You little squirt, I'll free your soul for you."

"About twenty," Maurice said.

He turned and walked out. Should he have told?

Did he have a choice?

The least he could do was ride back up there and tell how many Sundeen had. God – and watch their faces drop.

The photographer from Beuhman & Hartwell caught him outside on the steps and said, "If you're going back up, I'm going with you." Then Bill Wells of the St. Louis paper and several other reporters said they were going too. Then a man Maurice had never seen before came up and said, "Maurice, I've been looking for you. I'll be in your debt if you'll present me to Dana Moon and Captain Early."

Maurice was certain he had never seen the man before this. For how could he have forgotten him? The gleaming store teeth and waxed guardsman mustache twirled to dagger points –

"Colonel Billy Washington, at your service, Maurice."

– the pure-white Stetson, the tailored buckskin coat with white fringe, the black polished

295

boots with gold tassels in front –

"You've heard of me, have you?"

"Yes sir, I certainly have," Maurice said. God, all this happening at once. "I just have never seen you in person before."

"Well, you see me now," Colonel Washington said.

3

Bo Catlett rode up out of the barranca and crossed the open ground to the wall. He said to the people standing behind it, "They on the way."

"How many?" asked Bren.

"Say a hundred, give or take," Bo Catlett rode into the yard before stepping down, pulled his carbine from the boot and slapped his mount toward the smell of feed and water over in the corral.

"Five to one," Bren said, sounding pleased.

Kate looked at him, her Henry resting on the wall. Moon gazed down the slope, past the open ground to the trough of the barranca. He could see figures now, a line of tiny dark specks coming up the switchback trail, through the field of saguaro.

Bren raised the field glasses hanging from his neck and studied the enemy approaching. "Straggling . . . close it up there!"

Moon looked at his Apaches. They looked at him, faces painted now with streaks of ochre. He turned to look at the Mexicans lining the wall: Eladio with his sword and green sash among the farmers in white cotton.

"Tell 'em to get ready," Bren said, field glasses at his face.

"You don't have to stay," Moon said in Spanish. "No one is asked to fight one hundred men."

The Indians and the Mexicans remained at the wall, looking from Moon to the slope. They saw another of the colored men now, Thomas Jefferson, coming across the open ground and through the gate space in the wall.

"They dismounting, like to come as skirmishers."

Bren lowered his glasses and called out, "Come on! Take your medicine like little men! . . . Christ, what're they fooling around down there for?"

Moon said to Bo Catlett, "They'd do better to stay mounted and run at us."

"Man never soldiered," Bo said. "Can see he don't know doodly shit what he's doing."

The sound of firing came from down the

slope now . . . the tiny figures spreading out, moving up slowly, dropping down to fire, waiting, moving up again.

"Christ, it'll take 'em till tomorrow," Bren said. The Mexican farmers were raising their rifles. "Not yet," Moon said in Spanish. "If you shoot now I think they won't come close enough. We want them up there on the open ground."

"We get them up," Bo said.

"What's your signal?" Moon asked him.

"Three quick ones. My boys'll light the fuses and get."

Moon held his hand out. In a moment Bren noticed and handed him the glasses. Moon studied the figures coming up through the brush and fencepost saguaros. He raised his gaze to a high point on one side of the barranca, then moved across to the other side where the barranca narrowed and Bo Catlett's powdermen had planted the charges. The tiny figures dotting the slope were coming up through the narrowing of the trough and spreading out again, more of them firing now, the closest nearing two hundred yards. They could blow the charges now and wipe out about a quarter of Sundeen's men and send the rest running. But that wasn't the plan. No, Bren had promised Sundeen safe passage — one

298

general to another. That was all right. Because the plan was to get them all up on high ground, in the open, then blow the narrows and cut off their retreat, prevent them from falling back to cover. Get them milling around in the open and shoot the spirit right out of them, blow Sundeen to his reward and close the book. That was the plan.

The first skirmishers were approaching a hundred and fifty yards now, snapping shots and moving up, feeling the excitement of it probably, feeling braver with no one shooting back. Moon moved his glasses over them to pick out Sundeen. Not in the first bunch . . . there he was with his funneled hat and silver buckles, crossed gunbelts and a six-shooter in each hand, waving his men to come on, goddamn it, get up there.

Moon set the glasses on the wall and raised his Big-Fifty Sharps.

"Don't you do it," Bren said.

Moon said, "I'm just seeing how easy it would be."

"Let him come up all the way."

Pretty soon now.

The skirmishers were firing from a hundred yards and the tail end of Sundeen's men was moving through the narrows. The firing increased. Sundeen positioned a line of shooters behind cover, just across the open ground – about twenty of them, gave a signal and they all fired at once.

Seeing this about to happen, the people behind the wall ducked down or went to one knee. All except Bren Early. After the second fusillade he said, "At Fredericksburg, where Doubleday's Iron Brigade stood up to the Rebel guns, D.H. Hill sent a flag of truce over with his compliments to General Doubleday –"

Another volley ripped out from the brush slope. Bren tried not to hunch his shoulders.

"– saying he had never in his experience seen infantry stand and suffer casualties under artillery fire more bravely."

Moon said, "You have got something in your head about having to die to win glory. If that's the deal, I pass . . . Bo, let's close the back door. Give your troopers the signal."

Bren, standing, said, "Hold there," and pick up the glasses from the wall. "Some more are coming up behind."

Kate had said to Moon, "I'm not staying in the house; you know that." He said no, he guessed not. "But if you worry out there about me instead of yourself, you'll get shot. So think of me as another hand, not as a woman or your loved one." Moon had agreed because there was no fighting her. Though he had said, "If something happens to you, your old dad will kill me."

At the wall now Kate was alert, aware of being in the middle of men's business and would pick out little things that surprised or impressed her. The stoic look of the Apaches. Were they afraid? Was Eladio afraid? Yes, he looked it; but didn't leave when given the chance. Was Bren afraid, standing up to their rifle fire? Or was he beyond fear, playing his hero role? Bo Catlett and the other cavalryman – she thought of them as professional soldiers who would stand because that's what you did. Moon. Moon had good sense, he *must* be afraid. But his look was the same, his gaze, his unhurried moves, the hunk of tobacco in his jaw. She did not think of herself until the concentrated fire came from the slope and she crouched close to the adobe, feeling the pistol in the waistband of her skirt digging into her, clutching the Henry tightly and seeing her knuckles, close to her face, standing out white and hard. There was a feeling of terrible pressure. She could die on this spot . . . hearing Moon say if that was the deal he'd pass, saying it so calmly . . . all of them appearing calm as the rifle fire cracked and sang through the air. Determined, not resigned, but quiet about it.

You'd better be, huh? Was it that simple? Run and they'd shoot you in the back. It was fascinating, even with the feeling of pressure. The ultimate, a life or death situation. Bren said, "Hold there . . ." The firing stopped. They began to raise up from the wall.

"They're riding through Sundeen's people," Bren said. "They're not his. Some other bunch."

"That's your friend," Moon said. "What's his name."

"Maurice. Christ Almighty, one of 'em's leading a pack animal."

Kate could see the shooters who had been down in the scrub and rocks standing now, looking around, as this parade of single-file riders came through them led by Maurice Dumas . . . nine, *ten* of them, the packhorse carrying something covered with canvas, poles sticking out, bringing up the rear. They came across the open ground and now the second rider, wearing a tall white hat, drew even with Maurice in his cap. As Kate got a good look at the man she said, "My God," and turned to Moon who was staring at them and showing the first expression of pure surprise she had ever seen on his face.

The man in the white Stetson and fringed buckskin dismounted in the yard. Maurice, still

302

mounted, was saying something as the others rode into the yard behind him. The man in the white hat raised his hand to stop Maurice. "No need," he said, and walked over to Moon and Bren Early.

"Gentleman, I would know you anywhere. Even if I had not seen your renown C.S. Fly photographs I would know you are the famous scout, Dana Moon . . . and you, sir, Captain Brendan Early." He was taking something out of his fringed coat now — his false teeth and waxed handlebars agleam, something that looked like picture postcards in vivid colors, and said, "Gentlemen, may I present myself . . . Colonel Billy Washington, here to extend a personal invitation to both of you to join the world-famous Billy Washington All-American Wild West Show as star attractions and performers . . . *if*, of course, you get out of this jackpot you're in alive. What do you say, gents?"

Moon looked at Kate. Kate looked at Moon.
Bren was saying, "What —"
The man from Beuhman & Hartwell and his assistant were setting up their camera, both of them glancing up at the sun. The news reporters were looking around at the scenery and down the slope toward the skirmishers standing

303

in the scrub, judging the distance with keen gaze, beginning to make notes . . . the Mimbres, the Mexican farmers, the two black cavalrymen looking at the reporters and the bill-show man in the white hat and buckskins, staring at them. Where did they come from?

Bren was saying now, "Will you all kindly move out of the way? Go inside the house. Go on." Shooing them, going over to the photographer who was beneath his black cloth now. "Mister, will you move out of the way —"

Kate kept looking at Moon. She said, "What are we doing here?"

Moon didn't say anything; but his eyes held hers until they heard the voice call out from the slope.

"What in the hell's going on!"

Sundeen stood with several of his men at the edge of a brush thicket, looking up at the wall, at the people they could see close beyond the wall and through the gate opening. Now he yelled, "Get those people out of there!" and waved his arm.

"Jesus Christ," he said to the man in the derby hat next to him, who had been with Sundeen since the beginning of this company business, "you believe it?"

The man didn't say anything; he was squinting in the glare, frowning. The man didn't seem to know what to think.

"Goddamn it," Sundeen said, "give 'em a round."

When the man in the derby hat didn't move or raise his Winchester, Sundeen took the rifle from him, levered as he jerked it eye-level, fired, levered, fired . . . seeing them scatter now . . . levered and fired again, sending his shots singing off the adobe wall where some of them had been standing, then yelled, "We're coming up!"

He half turned and began waving to his men to come on. Not one of them moved. Sundeen pulled his hat off, stared, put his hat on again close over his eyes, pushed the rifle at the man in the derby hat, placed his hands on his hips and looked all around him at his mean Turks. They stood in the hot dusty scrub and shale watching him or looking up the slope.

Very slowly, Sundeen said, "What is going on?"

Before the man in the derby hat could answer — if he was going to — a voice from the yard yelled, "Hold your fire, I'm coming out!"

Sundeen watched the picture-taker and his assistant appear with their camera and heavy tripod, coming out of the yard and moving to a rise off to the side where they began to set up the equipment. Sundeen stared, pulling his funneled hat brim lower. As the picture-takers were getting ready, the man in the bill-show cowboy outfit appeared at the wall and called out, "Mr. Sundeen! —"

Sundeen let go, yelling now as loud as he could. "Get that fancy son of a bitch out of there!" Said, "Jesus," in his breath and started up the slope by himself.

Kate saw him first. She had begun to feel a letdown, a tired after-feeling; but now the pressure of fear returned. Looking around, she said, "Dana?"

No one was facing this way.

Only the young newsman, Maurice. Moon was over by the others, moving them toward the house. Kate thought, You have to hurry. They have to hurry. This is what they were waiting for. Bren was walking Billy Washington across the yard, the wild-west show impresario holding onto Bren's arm with one hand, gesturing with the other as he spoke, waving his arm in a wide arc to take in the world.

"Dana!"

Moon came around, alert to his wife's tone. He looked out toward the wall, his gaze holding as he came back toward the gate opening. He stood there, as if to greet Sundeen coming across the open ground.

Kate said, "Dana?"

He didn't look at her now. Kate turned to the wall where the Henry rifle rested on the flat surface, pointing out. She stood some fifteen feet from her husband.

Maurice stood between them, but several feet back from the wall. He didn't know if he should stay here. No one had said anything to him. Sundeen had reached the flat piece of ground beyond the wall. He was about fifty feet away now. Beyond Moon – and the group of Apaches and Mexican farmers spaced farther down the wall – on the rise off to the side, the photographer was fooling with his camera, the assistant holding open the black cloth for him to duck underneath. From Beuhman & Hartwell, Tucson. Maurice remembered that. He wasn't sure of the spelling though. Or how to spell the colored man's name – the two colored soldiers in their army braces and boots, off beyond Moon's wife. Sundeen's belt buckles glinted in the direct sunlight. Sundeen with a revolver on each hip, bullet belts crossed in an old-time desperado style . . . My God, was Moon armed? . . . Yes, the shoulder rig. He was in his shirtsleeves and wore braces and there seemed to be all manner of straps over his shoulders and around his back. Moon with a shoulder holster. Sundeen with his gun butts almost touching his hands hanging at his sides.

Did he say something? Mention Sonora?

Maurice could see all the hired manhunters waiting down there at the edge of the scrub. There was sky behind Sundeen's head and shoulders.

He said, "You first, Moon, then your friend. Where is he at?"

"He doesn't come right now," Moon said, "you'll never see him again."

This took place in moments, right before Maurice's eyes. Bren Early was somewhere behind him in the yard. Maurice wanted to turn around, but couldn't take his eyes off Sundeen . . . or Moon, he could see by shifting his eyes a little. He wanted to call out Bren Early's name, get him over here. But at this moment there was an awful silence. Two armed men facing each other. Was there a signal? Men shot each other from a distance or sneaked up or came into a place shooting if one wanted to kill another. Did this happen? Maybe it did, for it was certainly happening now, Maurice thinking: Before your very eyes.

Sundeen said, "Your move."

Maurice saw Moon's right hand cross his body.

He saw Sundeen's right hand with a revolver

in it. Like that. He saw the glint of sunlight on gun metal.

He heard an explosion, a heavy, hard report and a quick cocking lever action in the echo . . . to his left, where Kate Moon stood holding the big Henry rifle at her shoulder . . . and Sundeen was stumbling back, firing with a shocked look on his face, firing wildly again as Moon extended his revolver and fired and Kate fired the Henry, the two of them hammering Sundeen with .44's and that was the end of him. There was a silence. Sundeen lay on his back with his arms and legs spread out.

Maurice heard voices, someone in the yard calling out, running this way. He saw Kate lower the Henry and look at her husband, first with concern, then beginning to smile faintly. Moon looked over at his wife, not smiling but with a calm expression. Moon shook his head then. Maurice turned to see Bren Early coming with a matched .44 Russian in each hand.

Bren saying, "You got him? . . . You *got* him!" At the wall now, pointing a revolver down the slope and yelling at his men, his Apaches and Mexicans and pair of old cavalarymen, "Now! Pour it into 'em, boys!"

Moon turned away. Bren looked at him, a dumb, bewildered expression.

"We got to finish it!" All excited.

Moon shook his head. "You're too late for your glory." He looked at his wife. "When did it happen?"

Kate said, "I think it was over before it started."

"I guess so." Moon said then, "You shoot good for a little girl."

She said, "I wasn't gonna see you die for no reason."

Bren looked at them, from Moon to Kate and back. His gaze moved to Sundeen stretched face up on the bare ground and beyond him to the men standing in the scrub, Bren full of desperate energy brought to a halt.

"His people are still there . . . *look*."

But with little conviction in his tone. A last, too-late call to battle.

Remember it, Maurice thought. All of it:

Bo Catlett sitting on the wall, lighting a cigar. The other cavalry veteran leaning against it, his back to the scene of battle.

The Mimbre Apaches – gone. Where? Just gone. The Mexican farmers and the young one with the sword, moving away, walking off past the newsmen and the bill-show dude standing on the porch.

Moon gazing in that direction –

He said, "Well, we've paid up and lived to tell about it."

The bill-show man in buckskins was coming out toward them now, getting important-looking papers out of his pocket.

Moon watched him. He said to Bren, "It wouldn't hurt to travel, see the sights, would it?"

Kate shook her head, resigned or admiring or both. She said to Moon, "You're the sights. You and your partner."

Maurice Dumas got out his notebook and started writing it all down as fast as he could.

ABOUT THE AUTHOR

Elmore Leonard has written over fifteen novels and numerous short stories, several of which have been turned into successful films including *3:10 to Yuma* and *Valdez Is Coming*. He has also written the screenplays for such films as *Joe Kidd*, starring Clint Eastwood, and *Mr. Majestyk*, starring Charles Bronson. His novel, *Hombre*, was chosen as one of the twenty-five best Western novels ever written by the Western Writers of America and *The Switch*, published by Bantam, was nominated by the Mystery Writers of America for the Edgar Allan Poe Award for the best paperback of 1978.

Of his interest in the West, Mr. Leonard writes: "At the rail of a Missouri River steamboat Gary Cooper sees, for the first time, a man smoking a cigarette. He comments, 'Mister, your toothpick's on fire.' And before *The Plainsman* was over – and Porter Hall, the cigarette smoker, had shot Cooper in the back – I was hooked on Westerns forever. More inspiration came from *My Darling Clementine* and *Red River*. And finally, a year after *The Gunfighter* appeared, I was writing them myself. Curiously though, I'm inspired and motivated more by a novel that isn't a Western – though it seems to have the basic elements – than by traditional Western novels and motion pictures; and that's Hemingway's *For Whom The Bell Tolls*. But maybe it isn't so strange. The desire to write or read Westerns comes more from a feeling than a visual stimulus. Living in Detroit, as I do, wouldn't seem to be conducive. There sure aren't any buttes or barrancas out the window. But if you squint hard enough – wherever you are – you can see riders coming with Winchesters and Colt revolvers, and watch them play their epic roles in a time that will never die."